P9-DTN-305

ARTHUR, THE ALWAYS KING

For Elizabeth and Pippa Cook, with love
KC-H

For Jo
CR

Crossley-Holland, Kevin,
Arthur the Always King /
2023.

u   12/27/23

ARTHUR
THE ALWAYS KING

Kevin Crossley-Holland

ILLUSTRATED BY Chris Riddell

CANDLEWICK STUDIO
an imprint of Candlewick Press

‖ INTRODUCTION ‖

*Each of us must have a dream
to light our way through this dark world.*

How utterly amazing that, many centuries before anything ever went viral, King Arthur was recognized throughout Europe and beyond as the greatest of all heroes——so great that from the west of Wales to Syria and from Iceland to Sicily, and just about everywhere in between, hundreds and hundreds of stories and poems were written about him.

These stories and narrative poems, sometimes called romances, were inventions by medieval writers, and they have next to nothing to do with the obscure Celtic leader known as Artos or Arthur who lived during the sixth century. Between them, they show us

each stage of the legendary Arthur's life, beginning with his magical conception at Tintagel; his charmed childhood with his elder brother, Kay, in the west of England; his feat pulling the sword from the stone; and, when he was only fifteen, his crowning as the true-born king of England.

The stories about Arthur are just as popular today as they were eight hundred years ago, and so you may already know some of them. They describe how the young King Arthur assembled the finest knights in the kingdom to sit at the Round Table, where the names of their companions were Kindness, Friendship, Courtesy, Humanity, and Chivalry. At the heart of the Arthurian romances is the king's dream that there

‖ 2 ‖

could be a Golden Age such as the world had never seen before, so I have shaped this book to tell one story illustrating each stage of Arthur's dream, and the idea behind it.

We share each step in the king's quest: how he fought single-handed against the appalling giant of Mont-Saint-Michel; how he fell in love with beautiful Guinevere; and how the ageless magician Merlin counseled the young king, encouraged him and warned him, before destroying himself. There are romances about the incredible bravery of individual knights, such as Sir Gawain in his thrilling encounter with the Green Knight; passionate love matches; and the vital quest for the Holy Grail. All this, and then Sir Lancelot and Queen Guinevere's dramatic love affair, and the ghastly enmity of King Arthur with his own son.

The glory of Arthur's dream is that it's about human beings, not about gods or supermen and superwomen, but that is also its tragedy. These breathtaking, sometimes rollicking, sometimes lyrical, sometimes thought-provoking, and often witty stories are about us. Indeed, each romance says so much about ourselves that, like each generation, we need our own retelling and reshowing. Each of us will experience these stories in new, old ways: word and image working in harmony. Our dreams, our ambitions and limitations, our passions, our frustrations and disappointments, our resilience, they are all here. And each tale springs from a strong moral sense of what's right, what's wrong, and how we're all part of it.

After battling his own son, King Arthur vanishes, but he does not die. Combining so many insights into the medieval world with high imagination, these are the stories of a king and of a glorious dream still very much alive, alive for all generations and all times. That's why I've called this book *Arthur, the Always King.*

Kevin Crossley-Holland

|| CONTENTS ||

KING ARTHUR

SIR TRISTRAM

SIR GERAINT

SIR LANCELOT

SIR KAY

SIR GALAHAD

SIR GARETH

SIR GAHERIS

SIR GAWAIN

SIR BEDIVERE

SIR LAMORAK

SIR LUCAN

I

|| ARTHUR'S CHILDHOOD ||

Murk. Mud.

Flecks and pads of salt foam whisked up from the roaring ocean. They flew over the jagged sea cliff.

In the almost dark, a man who may have been young, maybe old, and probably both carefully picked his way along the path leading from the castle on the clifftop toward the little village of Tintagel. Just one slip or trip and he'd have been food for the fishes. Then the man tramped up the path from the village leading to the manor of Sir Ector, two miles inland.

Look! This man——his name is Merlin——is carrying something very, very small. Wrapped in a cloth of gold.

A swaddled baby no more than two or three days old.

A baby called Arthur.

||||||||||||||||||||||||||||||||||||

But Arthur's story begins nine months and a few days before this.

It begins when Merlin used magic to trick Arthur's mother, Ygerna, Duchess of Cornwall, into the arms of King Uther, who was passionately in love with her. The magician changed the king so that Uther looked and felt exactly like Ygerna's own husband, Gorlois.

So King Uther and Ygerna were spellbound, and Arthur was their son.

And what was the price Merlin agreed with Uther? Nothing less than this: Ygerna was to give her baby to Merlin as soon as he was born. She would entrust him to the magician without knowing

where Merlin was taking him, or who was looking after him, or even whether the child was still alive.

Merlin spirited the baby away from sobbing Ygerna and carried him, pink and small as a shrimp, to his foster parents.

So that is how this story really begins.

Or did it begin long before that? Was it a gleam in the magician's eye?

Merlin tramped through the dark hours when nightmares galloped through the starless sky, snorting and neighing.

Outside Sir Ector's gate, a lantern swung in the wind, like a shining truth assailed by the swarming dark.

A trustworthy knight, Sir Ector, with a capable wife, Margery, and a little son, Kay. A chunk of a farming man with an open smile who had a way of whistling back at the whistling choughs and curlews. A man who had learned to read and loved nothing more than to surround himself with candles and open a manuscript across his lap and tease out an old story.

The magician made a fist of his right hand and knocked at the hefty oak door.

Sir Ector and Lady Margery were ready. They had been waiting for this hour. Lady Margery herself swung open the door. At once, Merlin passed her the little parcel, and she cradled it and hurried away to Kay's nursery. She had decided not to farm the new baby out to a wet nurse in the village but to feed him herself.

But a world away, in a drafty castle room overlooking the welling and snatching sea, a voice was singing and sobbing:

"My son! My son!
Almost unbegun."

Little Arthur didn't know that. As he began to grow up, what he knew was that he was Sir Ector and Lady Margery's second son. Kay's younger brother.

||||||||||||||||||||||||||||||||||

Sir Ector's manor sat at the top of a tight valley between two hills, late to see the sunlight, quick to lose it. Sometimes the mist had a way of wrapping around it and clinging to it all day.

A stranger could strain his eyes, unsure whether or not he could make out the manor.

"We're in this world and out of it," Sir Ector pronounced with satisfaction.

"Or in this world and in another," his friend Merlin suggested with a smile.

"Between worlds," said Sir Ector.

"If I really had to live in any single place and time," Merlin told him, "I would choose your manor."

Outside roamed the huge black dog who howled at night and galloped away over the moorland, yes, and screeching night-hags, and the prowling ghost who patrolled the cliff path beyond the castle: beings living between times, and between waking and dreams.

But inside the manor house, with its mighty oak beams and moorstone walls, Arthur and Kay felt safe, and the magician often visited them there.

"What's what," the cook Jolly often told the two boys before they understood what she meant. "Yes, you two need to know what's what."

But as soon as they could understand anything, Arthur and Kay learned the difference between *can* and *can't* and *do* and *don't,* and the rules and rhythms of the manor.

When Arthur was six and his brother almost eight, Sir Ector told his sons, "What I want is to see you two working at your skills so that you'll become well-trained squires. Your fencing. Your tilting. Your wrestling. You haven't even ridden to hounds yet. And your archery. Most of your arrows not only miss the bull; they miss the target altogether. And talking of bulls, I want you both to share the work of everyone here in this manor and in our village."

"Like blacksmithing," said Arthur.

"Cooking," said Kay, sucking in his cheeks.

"Shearing."

"Mucking out the stables."

"Felling."

"Wringing the necks of chickens," said Kay. "I know——and if we hear a cock crowing, after noon, it's a death-omen and we have to kill him at once."

"Why?" asked Arthur. "Why do we have to do different kinds of work?"

"I'll tell you," said Sir Ector. "Think of a row of seven people with five people standing on their shoulders and three people standing on their shoulders, and——"

"I see," Arthur said. He flexed his knees and began to bounce.

"We all depend on each other," their father continued, wagging his finger at them. "And God assigns to each of us our responsibilities. You must learn what they are if you want to be squires, and that includes understanding what other people have to do."

"When will I become a squire?" Kay asked.

"When I see that you're ready to be," his father replied. "And Arthur too. When you've improved your skills and learned your duties. When you're fit in body and mind."

"When I'm eleven?" Kay pressed him.

"Maybe."

"Is it true," Kay asked his father, "that your sister, Lady Laudine, owns a townhouse in the City of London?"

"It is."

Then the boys started to yap around Sir Ector and beg him to take them to see her and the house and all the sights of London, but he would have none of it.

"Enough!" he said. "Now, then. Have either of you seen Merlin today? I need to speak to him."

No one ever knew where Merlin was. Not for long, anyhow. He had a way of entering or leaving a room without anyone noticing, and his idea of time was not the same as anyone else's.

"Time is what you make it," he told Arthur. "You can speed it up. Slow it down."

"You can't delay the sun rising," said Arthur. "Can you?"

Merlin just smiled.

Once, the boys asked Merlin whether he had ever ridden to London and met Lady Laudine.

"Have you really?"

"You've never told us."

"Are the streets made of gold?"

"Did you see a dancing bear?"

"Is it true some houses are five levels high?"

"What were you doing there?"

When the boys sang in tune——instead of getting in each other's way, as they often did——Merlin felt as if he were being pelted with snowballs so thick and fast that he had no time to throw one himself.

He held up his hands.

"London shall mourn the death of twenty thousand and the Thames will be turned to blood," he announced in a loud solemn voice.

Arthur and Kay looked up at him, startled.

"What is the Thames?" Arthur asked.

"I will tell you about the giant hedgehog loaded with apples, and the heron, and the snake encircling London with its long tail. I will, but not today."

"Merlin!" cried the boys.

"You know your father," Merlin said. "He needs to see me, and he believes time never waits."

"But what do you mean? Twenty thousand . . . a giant hedgehog."

"I can tell you old prophecies," Merlin replied. "I can't tell you meanings. If you need to know meanings, you'll have to find them out for yourselves."

|||||||||||||||||||||||||||||||||||||

The two boys were as curious as they were eager, and usually they were good companions. By the time Arthur was seven and Kay was nine, they sometimes played hooky and risked the consequences. More than once, they trekked toward the far moors and stuffed their leather shoulder bags with their findings——stones so perfectly round they could play marbles with them, bones of stoats and weasels and little birds, crystals as small as their fingertips. Once, they found a deserted stone chamber, half underground, and crawled into it, and frightened themselves with horrible stories. Then the mist came down like a sopping blanket.

The boys peered into it, trying to decide which way to go. That was no good, though. They had to huddle in the stone chamber all night, and Kay tried to hide his own fear by taunting his younger brother and accusing him of being afraid. When they got back to the manor next morning, they saw their mother weeping for the first time, and, angry because they'd left the manor without his permission, their father thrashed them.

What Arthur and Kay liked to do most of all was what Sir Ector had absolutely forbidden: cliff-fishing. They used to walk along the clifftop path beyond the castle. There they tied hooks to their lengths of line and baited the hooks with scraps of raw meat they had begged off Jolly. Then they wedged themselves between two rocks and lowered their lines fifty feet, one hundred feet, one hundred and forty-three feet down to the water. And each boy threaded his line between his big toe and second toe or gripped it between his teeth, so that he would feel it the moment he had a bite.

Oh, what glory! The colored butterflies fluttering around them, the field birds singing and the sea birds squawking . . . and then the bite and the long haul, and peering over the edge to see what they had caught, and feeling quite dizzy at the sight of the sea swaying and fizzing so far beneath them. Mackerel, herring, sea trout, green and gold and gaping . . .

But once, a sea monster snapped at Kay's tasty bait, and the line between his teeth suddenly tightened and whipped sideways and ripped his right cheek.

Kay yelped. His blood spurted up into his eyes and pumped over his right ear, down his chin and neck. Then he became frightened and tried to stand up without being able to see, but Arthur hauled him down again, wiped away the blood with his sleeves, and shepherded him back along the cliff edge path to safety.

Later that day, Merlin led the boys to the wise woman in the village and she stitched the two fillets of Kay's right cheek together with some of his own sisal fishing line. Then she boiled

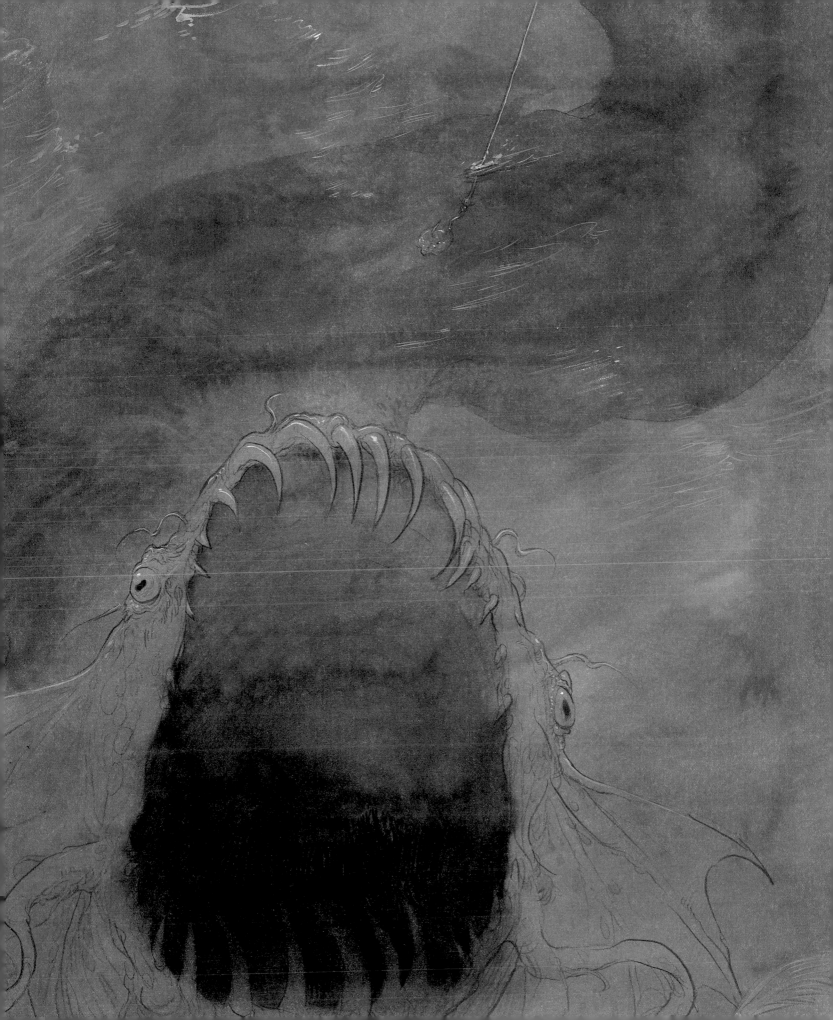

herbs and crushed them into a poultice and smeared it onto Kay's face to reduce the swelling. After that she warbled something not even the magician could understand.

Sir Ector was mightily disapproving of Kay for disobeying him and for causing his own injury.

"There's an old story about that," he grumbled. "About a squire who tried to run before he could walk. Yes, and about a dwarf and a very strange beast. I'll tell you, one day."

Sir Ector praised his younger son, though. "You remained calm, Arthur, and led Kay back safely. You were loyal. He was able to depend on you."

"Kay would have done the same," Arthur replied.

Sir Ector glared at his elder son. "Would you, Kay?" he demanded. "Well, that scar is with you for life."

| | | | | | | | | | | | | | | | | | | | | | | | | |

When Kay or Arthur thought Sir Ector had been unfair or too heavy-handed, they sometimes turned to Lady Margery, not for kisses or caresses——she had none of those——but for brisk good cheer.

In the way some people come to look like their faithful dogs or the horses they have ridden for many years, Lady Margery's face was like a ripe pink pear growing on one of her pleached fruit trees: beneath her braided golden topknot, her forehead was somewhat narrow while her jowls were rather baggy.

But the boys soon learned to be careful when their mother walked them out into her beloved garden, and both knew what it was to be snared into spreading manure or hoeing or weeding for hour after hour.

"Do you know that bees sleep on the wing?" she asked them. "And do you know how to go to war with ants, and how to drive them out of the garden? And what about germinating rosemary?" She veritably bubbled around, singing little snatches as she went:

*"I turned to wander at mine ease
Beneath the burgeoning
mulberry trees..."*

Lady Margery laughed. "Not that there's much ease or wandering in my garden," she said. "I know! Now, you two, have I told you how to find a pearl inside one of these apples? Ah! And look at this lily... There's a story about every plant and tree. Dozens of old stories!"

While both boys came to understand a great deal about the magic of everyday wonders, the language of the birds and colors of their eggs, and the astonishing gossamer spun by spiders across cropped grass before dawn, and how there were magic charms you could whisper in a horse's ears to quiet or excite it, and hundreds of such things, they really knew very little about the world beyond Sir Ector's manor and the nearby village.

By the time they were nine and eleven, there was little they hadn't heard about carving game——how to

tame a crab and splat a pike and unjoint a bittern, disfigure a peacock and unlace a rabbit——but apart from one day-long journey with Sir Ector to swear loyalty to Leodegrance, King of Camelerd, they almost never strayed far from home. It was at Camelerd, though, that Arthur first met the king's only daughter, who was a year younger than he was. And for the first time in his life, he felt his heart quicken because of a girl.

On their way back from Camelerd, Sir Ector told his two sons about Lyonesse, the sunken land between Cornwall and the Scilly Isles, and how it had all been drowned during an enormous sea surge, and how you could still hear the bells of its churches pealing beneath the waves.

"Have you heard them?" asked Arthur.

"I have," Sir Ector replied. "They sounded far, far away, like memories."

The boys were all for turning their horses around there and then, and riding west to the land's end so they could hear the bells for

themselves. But Sir Ector was having none of it.

"We're still the wrong side of Slaughter Bridge," he said, "and if we don't press on, the dark will reach the manor before we do."

As the months and seasons passed, Merlin continued to come and go, and twice he galloped into the manor courtyard accompanied by a posse of knights, to talk with Sir Ector, but their father had no intention of telling the boys why, and soon enough they forgot about the visits. Thrice the boys accompanied Lady Margery to the Lammas Fair, where they dodged to and fro between the animal pens and vegetable stalls, sat at the feet of a man playing the hurdy-gurdy, and marveled at all the wonders for sale: the woad and wine and sacks of wool, the furs of kids and cats and squirrels, linen spun from flax, and canvas and leather gloves and purses. And more than four times Arthur and Kay rode over to the monastery where the monks opened ancient manuscripts telling the history of Britain, written in Latin, and translated sentences from them, recounting how Brutus the Trojan became King of Britain, or Albion as it used to be called, and how Princess Cordelia truly loved her father, Leir, unlike her two loathsome sisters, Goneril and Regan.

Arthur and Kay watched spellbound while a young monk in the scriptorium mixed egg white and precious saffron into a kind of sticky golden glue and decorated the margins of a parchment page with some of the sea creatures you can find round the coast of Cornwall——seals and swans and singing dolphins and mermaids.

Once, twice, thrice, more than four times, and then at Christmas and Epiphany and Easter and several feast days of Cornish saints, Kay and Arthur accompanied their parents to the chapel inside the castle at Tintagel.

This was where Arthur first saw Ygerna without knowing she was his own mother. He had never questioned that he was Sir Ector and Lady Margery's younger son.

And it was there, too, that Arthur saw his three half sisters, the daughters of Ygerna and Gorlois: beautiful Morgan, who was only two years older than he was, and her elder sisters, Morgause and Elaine.

But after the chapel service, Sir Ector always hurried Arthur away, knowing how children sometimes open their mouths and ask awkward questions or spill out secrets without even knowing they are doing so.

Nevertheless, Arthur and Morgan were attracted to each other, and when he was fourteen and she was sixteen, their desire to meet was stronger than any obstacles in their way. Several times, Arthur went out riding on his own, and Morgan went out riding on her own, and they met secretly, not knowing they were half brother and half sister.

So time passed, as time does, and when Arthur was almost fifteen, Merlin brought the news to Tintagel, and to Sir Ector's manor, that King Uther had drunk water from a spring at Saint Albans that had been poisoned by his enemies, and died on the spot.

"I was there," said Merlin. "I was by the side of the king at Saint Albans with all his close followers."

"You were there," repeated Sir Ector.

"I was!" repeated Merlin. "Much as I relish your and Lady Margery's company and Jolly's excellent cooking, I can't stay here in Cornwall the whole time. Before the king died, I asked him: 'Sire, will your son become king? The next king of the realm of Britain?'"

The magician looked around at everyone to be quite sure they were hanging on his words.

"King Uther gasped. 'That is the law and custom of our land,' he said. 'Let him claim the crown. I give my trueborn son God's blessing.' Those were his last words."

"His trueborn son," said Arthur. "Who is he, then?"

"And how can he claim it?" asked Kay.

"Yes, what will he have to do?" Arthur persisted.

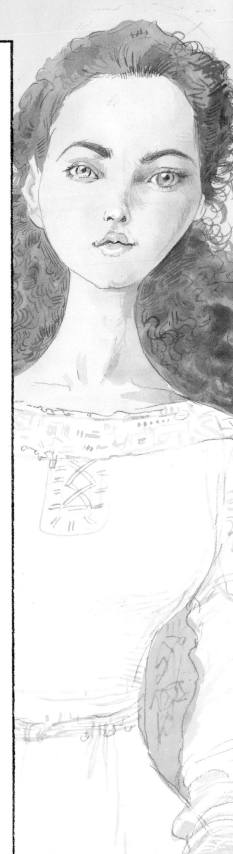

"Many simple questions have no simple answers," Sir Ector said, and he shook his head.

During King Uther's lifetime, the men and women of Britain had been of one mind and heart in repelling the invaders who declared it was nothing but a rebellious island and that they meant to reclaim it for the Roman Empire. Those were years of peace. But soon after the king's death, the dukes and earls and counts and lords and knights began to squabble, and there was no one to stop them.

All over the country, innocent travelers were murdered and armed groups of men stole gold and silver plate from monasteries.

Sir Ector did his utmost to shield his manor from all of it——the greed, the lust for power, the horrible disregard for human life, and the contempt even for God Himself.

"Britain is tearing herself to pieces," he told his sons. "She is turning herself into a wasteland. And the wrongs are so widespread, so terrible, that they can never be righted until our country has a new king."

||||||||||||||||||||||||||||||||||||

During the middle of October, the Archbishop of Canterbury dispatched riders north and east and west, carrying a message summoning all the knights in the country to London. He instructed them to come at midday on Christmas Eve to the church of Saint Paul's, where Jesus himself would perform a miracle to reveal to them their rightful king.

When he heard this message, Sir Ector said to Merlin, "Well, magician, you stood beside King Uther while he was dying and when he declared that his trueborn son must claim the crown."

"I did," Merlin agreed.

"So now I suppose you've been

whispering in the Archbishop of Canterbury's right ear——"

"Left ear," Merlin corrected him. "He's deaf in his right ear!"

Both boys looked at Merlin, startled.

Sir Ector pursed his mouth and shook his head. "What a storyteller you are, Merlin," he said, and he burst out laughing. "Anyone who didn't know you might really believe you."

Merlin compressed his lips. "Those most close to us are often the most blind," he replied. "At any rate, I presume you'll ride to London."

"We will, won't we?" chimed the boys.

"I know my duty," Sir Ector said.

"And it's my duty to accompany you," Merlin told him.

"If we're really going to have to ride up to London," Sir Ector said, "at least we can go to the New Year's tournament."

"Jousting!" shouted Kay. "And tilting and——"

"Not so fast!" his father said. "You're not allowed to take part unless

you're a knight . . ." Sir Ector sniffed. He turned away from the boys, glanced out of the little window, and scratched the top of his head. "Well, Kay," he said, and turned to face his elder son again, "I have been thinking for some months that it's about time I knighted you."

Kay threw up his arms for joy.

"You know all the responses, don't you?" his father asked.

"You've taught them to me."

"And you're sixteen, aren't you?"

"Rising seventeen."

"Just so," said Sir Ector.

"I'll be turning fifteen on our way up to London," Arthur added.

Kay's face was very pink——all except the dark-purple scar across his right cheek. He drew himself up to his full height, a little shorter actually than his younger brother, and smirked at Arthur.

"You can be my squire," he told him.

"No," Sir Ector said sharply, "Arthur is my squire, and a very

good one too. You'll only be entitled to your own squire after five years." Sir Ector smiled at his elder son. "All right, Kay! We must send for Lady Ygerna's priest to lead us to the chapel and to stand witness and bless you."

And that's what Sir Ector did. Jolly's old husband, Lovel, who was in charge of Lady Margery's vegetable garden, trundled down to the castle to fetch the priest, and in the meantime Jolly sharpened her sharpest carving knife and shaved off all the hair on the top of Kay's head, so that he had a bald spot almost as big as a kneecap.

By the time Lovel returned with Lady Ygerna's priest, Lady Margery had found the dusty white and rusty-red cloak in which Sir Ector himself had been knighted more than thirty years before, had given it a fearful shaking, and had dressed Kay in it.

Then she used Jolly's carving knife to stab a new hole in Sir Ector's old white belt.

"You're not as . . . sturdy as your father," she told him, shaking her head.

Arthur grinned. "You're skinny," he said.

"You're jealous," Kay replied.

"No," Arthur said. "Only skinny people get jealous."

The priest led the way to the chapel, which was little more than an alcove, really, on one side of the hall, and he and Sir Ector stood with their backs to the altar with Kay in front of them.

"You wish to become a knight," Sir Ector began.

Kay inclined his head. "I wish to follow my father's example," he said. "To protect the people here in this manor and in the village of Tintagel, who cannot protect themselves. To say what I believe to be right and to oppose what I believe to be wrong, wherever I ride. To serve Jesus with my head, heart, and body for as long as I live."

Then Kay got down onto his left knee. Sir Ector grasped the sword lying on the altar and tapped his son's right shoulder with it three times.

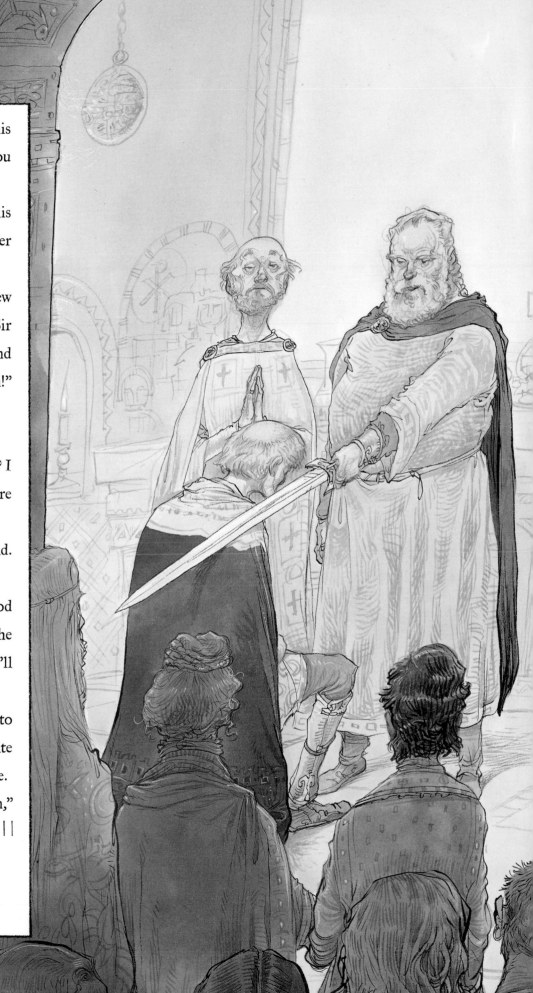

"I dub you knight," he said, and his voice sounded quite hoarse. "I dub you knight, Sir Kay."

Then the priest pronounced his blessing, and Lady Margery wiped her eyes, and the ritual was over.

Arthur turned to Kay and threw his arms around his elder brother. "Sir Kay!" he said rather admiringly. And then he turned to Sir Ector. "London!" he exclaimed. "When will we set off?"

"As soon as we can."

"And where will we stay on the way? I mean, how long will it take? And where will we actually stay in London?"

"With my sister," Sir Ector said. "Lady Laudine."

"We'll be at Saint Paul's in good time," Merlin assured Arthur, and the corners of his mouth twitched. "We'll slow down the hours if we need to."

Not for the first time, listening to the magician, the boys didn't know quite what to believe and what not to believe.

"Yes, as soon as we possibly can," Sir Ector said. ||||||||||||||||||||

|| MERLIN AND THE SWORD IN THE STONE ||

Sir Ector, the newly knighted Sir Kay, and Arthur set off for London during the third week of November, accompanied by Merlin.

A gentle west wind helped them on their way, and the soft sun warmed their backs.

"I never knew," said Arthur, "that Britain was so large. I didn't know there were so many hamlets and villages. Woods and hills and sandy heaths . . . I never knew about the old cobbled roads. Did you know there were so many bridges?"

"And tolls," Sir Ector added sharply.

"I never knew it was all so different," Arthur went on. "I never knew!"

"We get the idea, Arthur," his father said.

"And so wonderful!" Arthur exclaimed, throwing his arms as wide as the world.

"Christmas at home," Sir Ector grumbled. "That's what's wonderful." He sniffed. "My sister lives alone. There'll be no boar's head. No wassail. No kissing bough. I only hope Margery remembers the holly."

"You reminded her often enough," Merlin said.

"I don't want the manor overrun with witches. Rats and mice are bad enough."

The four travelers only reached the townhouse belonging to Lady Laudine on the afternoon of the day before Christmas Eve.

And what with stabling their horses, and washing away the worst

of the journey with rags and buckets of cold water, and eating, and sleeping, and dressing himself, and then airing his father's clothing in front of the fire and dressing him in his socks and leggings and doublet and breeches and cloak, and all the time trying to answer Lady Laudine's dozens and dozens of questions about Cornwall and their journey, Arthur could later remember only half of what had happened before they left for Saint Paul's on Christmas Eve morning.

It wasn't at all far to the great church, but such a crowd of people was converging on it that Sir Ector and his sons and Merlin had to shuffle along at the same slow pace as everyone else.

Kay kept smoothing down his clothing and proudly grasping the pommel of his new sword, now and then half drawing it and inspecting it.

"Why do you keep doing that?" Arthur asked him.

"Because . . ." Kay replied airily. "Because I can, Arthur!"

Arthur was much too fascinated by all the people around him to be put out. There were dukes and earls and counts and lords and knights and squires, as well as all the commoners of London, men and women and their sons and daughters, and he kept breaking his step to look at them. Then he saw a man carrying a large bunch of mistletoe and turned around to ask Merlin what the mistletoe was for . . .

But Merlin wasn't there. He had disappeared.

"Where is he?" Arthur exclaimed.

Sir Ector and his sons tried to spy the magician over the bobbing heads and caps of everyone around them.

"Drat!" complained Sir Ector in a gruff voice.

"He's done this before," Arthur said, "but when I ask him where he's been, he just smiles."

"No," said Kay. "No one can just disappear."

"Merlin lives by different rules from us and everyone else," Sir Ector observed. "You should know that by now. But really! Where is he?"

"Mistletoe! Mistletoe!" called the man in a reedy voice. "A sprig of the thunder-plant for a penny. Good luck for a penny!"

"Can we?" asked Arthur.

"Certainly not," Sir Ector replied. "We can't take mistletoe into a church."

"It's a heathen plant, Arthur," his brother told him. "My mother said so."

Saint Paul's was cavernous and gloomy and thick with sweet incense. And by the light of hundreds and hundreds of candles, Arthur could see that the press of people inside was even greater than outside.

All around him, men were hoisting banners and brandishing shields: blood orange and jasmine, gold, royal blue, sky blue and midnight blue, scarlet and black, celadon. And then Arthur saw that each raised shield and waving colored banner had its own design: three zigzags of sizzling lightning, or two swords, or five silver stars, or a harp, or a heart, or a golden lion rampant.

"The colors and patterns all have meanings," Sir Ector told the boys, "and because of them, you can recognize a knight when he's fully armed."

"In battle, you mean," said Sir Kay.

"Why are your shield and banner blue?" Arthur asked his father.

"We call it azure, the French word, and it stands for piety and sincerity."

"Why has it got keys on it?" asked Sir Kay.

"They signify good stewardship," his father replied, "and the keys of heaven. It was my father's before me, and it can be yours too."

Everywhere there was a humming: like a great swarm of honey bees in a wildflower meadow. It rose above Arthur's head and hovered over him.

"Here," said Sir Ector in his younger son's right ear, "you see the power and might of all Britain."

"It makes my blood tingle," Arthur said.

"It makes me tremble," his father replied.

Whenever Sir Ector recognized a banner or a shield, he pointed it out to the

boys. "There! That's Sir Lancelot's——the one with three scarlet stripes."

"Why the stripes?" asked Arthur.

"Because he's as strong as three strong men. He's been the champion of many tournaments and he's the strongest, most skillful swordsman in Britain. And there, that one with a falcon. That's Sir Geraint. His manor's in Devon, not so far from ours. And over there, can you see that older man with only one arm? That's Sir Bedivere. A great man! A loyal man. The very best of companions!"

Under his breath, Arthur began to mouth the words "or, argent, gules, sable, vert, azure, purpure."

"What's that?" asked Kay.

"The seven tinctures."

"What do you mean?"

"Don't you remember? The monks taught us their names: the seven colors used by the knights for the pictures and patterns painted on their shields and sewn on their banners?"

"Yes," said Kay. "To declare who they are and what they stand for."

"And on their horses' trappings too," Arthur added. "Or is gold and it stands for ambition, and argent is silver and it stands for peace, and gules is red and . . ."

"Yes, Arthur," Kay said impatiently. "I remember as well as you do."

Now and then, in one quarter of the church or another, the humming rose to an angry buzzing, then slowly died down again, but it only stopped completely when the Archbishop of Canterbury, robed in white, climbed into the pulpit and repeatedly pounded its oak paneling with his fist.

"How dare you bring your arguments and disagreements into this sacred space?" he demanded. "Ever since King Uther was buried, you've been tearing our island to pieces. Yes, all you powerful and mighty men of Britain. Arguing, stealing, skirmishing, murdering. Why? You know why." The archbishop angrily clapped his hands. "Because of your greed. Because you want more. More land.

More money. More followers. More power."

The archbishop's voice boomed and echoed around the vast church.

"You know why I've summoned you all to London," the archbishop continued. "We must find our new leader. Our rightful king. We owe it ourselves, we owe it our children, and we owe it to God to heal Britain and make our country whole again. And I believe"——the archbishop drew himself up, raised his right arm and slowly made the sign of the cross——"I believe Christ Himself will help us. I believe He'll help us with a miracle. Amen."

With a great deal of creaking and clanking, the great men of Britain got down onto their knees on the cold December stone and made their confessions. And then the mass priests walked among them, giving them wafers of bread and red wine——the body and blood of Jesus Christ.

As soon as Arthur and his brother and Sir Ector emerged from Saint Paul's, screwing up their eyes at the

bright early-afternoon light, they heard shouting and then they got caught in a press of people surging around the side of the church.

Close to the east wall, there was a plinth of shining white marble. On the middle of the plinth stood a massive steel anvil. And sticking into the anvil was a sword.

When Arthur balanced himself on the stone footing of the church wall, he was able to make out the lettering, enriched with gold, cut into the side of the plinth:

WHOSO PULLETH OUT
THIS SWORD FROM
THIS STONE AND
ANVIL IS RIGHTWISE
KING TRUEBORN OF
ALL ENGLAND

In slack-jawed silence, the great men of the country stared at the shining plinth, wondering where it had come from and who had placed it there.

The birds of London cried out with hoarse voices.

One thought after another chased through the men's minds like the little clouds scudding high above them, trying to catch up with each other. Opportunity, risk, trickery, magic, danger . . .

Arthur didn't think any of those things. He simply stared at the gold lettering. RIGHTWISE KING TRUEBORN. TRUEBORN . . .

"Well!" exclaimed a voice. "Who dares never loses. Who dares sometimes wins."

The voice belonged to Sir Lancelot.

Everyone considered him the strongest of them all. He was not only the most skillful swordsman but also the most generous to friend and enemy and the quickest to come to the aid of the powerless. No one disputed his right to be first.

Sir Lancelot stepped up onto the plinth. "Nothing comes of nothing," he announced. Then he grasped the pommel of the sword, braced himself, and pulled. But he couldn't shift the sword. Not one inch.

Sir Lancelot growled. "Again!" he muttered.

But the sword remained buried in the anvil.

"Again!" shouted Sir Lancelot.

For the third time, the greatest knight in Christendom tried with all his might to draw the sword from the anvil. But he could not.

TRUEBORN, thought Arthur. Wouldn't that mean the king's own son? Blood of his blood? It can't just mean a man as brave and strong as King Uther was, else Lancelot would have easily freed the sword.

Nevertheless, following Sir Lancelot, one knight after another tried his hand. One-armed Sir Bedivere and his brother Sir Lucan and the great jouster Sir Lamorak and eager young Sir Geraint from Devon and Sir Accolon of Gaul and Sir Balin from Northumberland——but not one of them was able to shift the sword.

"You've all been waiting for me," a voice called out. It was the jester, Sir Dagonet, who had never once fought in the field and mocked everyone who did.

"Laugh if you like!" he said, pushing his way through the crowd. "The last laugh may be on you."

Sir Dagonet grasped the shining pommel, but when he braced himself and tugged, it slipped right out of his hands and he fell over backward.

Everyone laughed and cheered.

Sir Dagonet dusted himself off. "You windbags!" he called out. "You pretenders and popinjays! Well, at least you know how to laugh."

Then an old knight, wearing a raggy black coat several sizes too large for him, shuffled forward.

"That's Sir Breunor le Noir," Sir Ector told Arthur. "He's strong, all right. Muscular. Strong enough to have killed a lion."

"But even if he is," protested Arthur, "he can't be trueborn. Not if that means blood of the king's blood. He's too old."

"Trueborn!" a man called out from the other side of the plinth. "Trueborn. That's what I heard King Uther say before he died at Saint Albans."

"I recognize that voice," Sir Ector said.

"It's Merlin!" exclaimed Arthur. "There! I can see him."

"I might have known," Sir Ector said with a sigh, and knitted his shaggy eyebrows.

"Trueborn is what the words say, at least to those of you who can read," the magician continued, loud and scornful. "So how can any knight here claim to be the son of King Uther?"

| | | | | | | | | | | | | | | | | | | | | | | | | | | | | | | | | | | | |

After Sir Breunor had tried and failed, the Archbishop of Canterbury appointed a guard of ten knights to stand watch day and night over the sword in the stone and to permit any knight to step up on the marble plinth to try his hand. Many did try, but not one of them could shift the sword.

On the day after Christmas, the feast of Saint Stephen, the first Christian martyr, many of the knights worshipped again at Saint Paul's, and then they hurried around to the sword in the stone. Some knights and their squires ranged through the city streets, following the wren hunters; some drank from wassail bowls in dingy taverns, and laughed and boasted, and sang carols; some crossed the great bridge built by the Romans and viewed the City of London from the other side of the river; some watched plays performed in the streets by masked actors playing the parts of the devil Beelzebub and Old Man Winter and Saint George and a dragon; and on the following day almost all of them fasted before returning again to Saint Paul's on Childermas to remember how cruel King Herod had murdered all the innocent babies in Bethlehem, wrongly believing that Jesus would be one of them.

That is how the last days of the old year drifted away.

Then the new year dawned, and with it new resolutions, new promises, new hopes——above all that King Uther's trueborn son, whoever he was and

wherever he was, would step forward and pull the sword from the stone.

On New Year's Day, a great tournament was held outside the city walls. Many knights rode out to tilt and joust and fight.

"I've told you about jousting before," Sir Ector said to his sons. "It's a dangerous game in which you fight and try to capture another knight's horse or a piece of his armor while he's trying to capture yours."

"I'll do that," Arthur said at once.

"You'll do nothing of the kind," his father replied. "You're a squire, not a knight."

Kay smiled a superior smile. "I am," he said. "I'll joust."

Such were the crowds of knights and their retinues, and all the commoners, that Arthur and Kay were soon separated from their father, and then they lost sight of him altogether.

The two of them rode side by side, astonished at all the armed knights and taking in the clanking, the neighing, the smell of leather, the

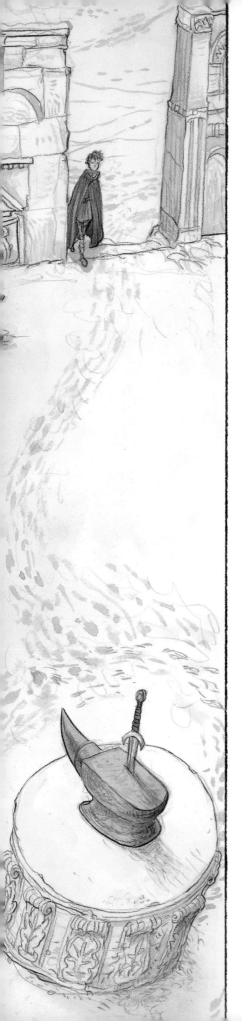

waving banners and colored shields, the hubbub. They felt overcome with excitement.

Kay turned his head this way and that way, trying to take it all in.

"You look like an owl," Arthur told him. "You'll screw your head right off if you're not careful."

"I'm going to joust," Kay said in a loud voice. He filled his lungs. "I'm going to joust!" Then he reached for his sword and looked around.

"What?" asked Arthur. "What's wrong?"

"Where is it?" Kay anxiously looked to left and right and then right under his horse as if he could have dropped it. "My sword. I must . . . I must have left it behind."

"How could you have?" said Arthur. "You slept with it lying alongside you."

"Your horse is faster than mine," Kay said to his brother. "Will you ride back and get it for me?"

"I will," said Arthur. "As quickly as I can."

So Arthur galloped all the way back to Lady Laudine's house, but she wasn't there, nor were any of her servants. They had gone to the tournament to drink mulled wine, eat minced meat pies, and enjoy the fighting and jousting, so all the doors were locked.

"No!" Arthur heard himself saying. "My brother can't do without a sword. He cannot and he shall not."

Then Arthur rode across to Saint Paul's churchyard, and there was no one else there. The changing guard of knights protecting the sword in the stone had gone to the tournament field along with everyone else.

Arthur dismounted and tied his horse to the churchyard gate.

He stepped up onto the marble plinth. And then, watched only by half a dozen curious pigeons and a couple of hares, he grasped the shining pommel. He gripped the cross guards. Lightly and fiercely, he pulled the sword out of the anvil.

|||||||||||||||||||||||||||||||||||

The moment Kay saw the sword, he knew it was not his own.

He knew it was the sword in the stone. At once, he rode around and around the tournament field until he found his father.

"Look!" he shouted. "Father! The sword in the stone! I'm the king—— the trueborn king."

Sir Ector looked Kay in the eye. "Follow me!" he instructed his son, and he spurred his horse.

Sir Ector rounded up Arthur and led both his sons straight back to Saint Paul's and strode into the church.

Then Sir Ector told Kay to lay his right hand on the Bible. "How did you get this sword?" Ector demanded.

Kay hesitated. "I . . . well, Arthur gave it to me."

Sir Ector looked Arthur in the eye. "And you? How did you get this sword, Arthur?"

"I went to Lady Laudine's house to find Kay's sword but there was no one there. So I said to myself, 'My brother can't do without a sword. He cannot and he shall not.' So I rode here, straight from your sister's house . . ."

"And then?" asked Sir Ector.

"I pulled this sword out of the stone."

"Was anyone here?"

Arthur half smiled. "Well, only lots of pigeons and a couple of hares."

Sir Ector led his sons out of the church and over to the marble plinth.

"Now, Arthur," he said. "Let me see you sheathe this sword and we will try to draw it out again."

Arthur sheathed the sword in the anvil.

"I'll try first," Sir Ector said, then he seized the sword and gave it such a tug that Arthur and Kay could hear his muscles cracking, but he couldn't shift it at all.

Sir Ector turned to Kay. "Now you try."

But Kay couldn't shift the sword either.

Then it was Arthur's turn. He stepped

up onto the plinth and firmly grasped the sword. He drew it lightly and fiercely from the anvil and held it up for them all to see. He waved the blade at high heaven. At once, Sir Ector and Kay got down on their knees.

"No!" said Arthur. "No!" And he pulled them back to their feet again.

"You are the trueborn king," Sir Ector told Arthur. He filled his old lungs with air and slowly, very slowly, let it all out again. "I am not your father," he explained, "but your foster father. Lady Margery is your foster mother. You and I are not of one blood."

Arthur felt flushed. He felt feverish.

Then Sir Ector told the boys how the magician Merlin had brought Arthur to the manor as a tiny baby, dressed in a cloth of gold, when he was only two or three days old. "I've never known for sure," he said, "but I've often wondered."

Tears welled in Arthur's eyes. "But you and Lady Margery..." he began. "You've fed me and loved me and taught me. I owe you more, much more, than anyone else in this wide world. And even if all this

is true, even if I'm crowned king, you can always and always ask me whatever you wish, and I'll never fail you."

"One thing only, sire," Sir Ector said. "Will you make Sir Kay, my own son, the steward of all your lands and estates?"

Arthur looked at Kay, who slightly lowered his head.

"I will," he said. "Of course I will. For better, for worse, Sir Kay will be my steward for as long as I live."

||||||||||||||||||||||||||||||||||||||

When all the dukes and earls and counts and lords and knights returned from the tournament field and heard what had happened, they were scornful and angry.

"Impossible!" they shouted.

"Out of the question."

"A beardless boy."

"He's not even a knight."

"It's a trick."

But seeing Arthur so calmly pull the sword from the stone again and again, and unable to do so themselves, a few of them accepted that he was indeed their trueborn king.

"But how can it be?" others demanded. "How can he possibly be the son of King Uther?"

Merlin counseled Arthur to be patient. "Time solves many mysteries. And reasonable people do change their minds."

After three days, the Archbishop of Canterbury made it known that he intended to knight and then to crown Arthur. Hearing this, many more knights decided to give him their support, including some of the greatest in the kingdom——Sir Lancelot, Sir Lamorak, Sir Bedivere, Sir Baudwin, Sir Ulfius, Sir Brastias. For all that, almost as many returned north and east and south and west, resentful and rebellious.

"You're going to need me, sire," Sir Dagonet told Arthur.

"Why is that?" Arthur asked his jester.

"You, our king? Aged fifteen. What a joke!"

Arthur made as if to clout the jester around the head but intentionally missed.

In the middle of January, the feast on the eve of Arthur's knighting and coronation, held at the young king's castle, Camelot, was interrupted by a messenger from King Rience of North Wales. This man told Arthur that Rience wore a cloak trimmed with the beards of eleven kings and needed just one more beard—— Arthur's beard——to complete the trimming.

"I'm only fifteen," Arthur told the messenger. "My

beard is still too soft to make a good trimming. Tell King Rience to come and get down on his knee bones and do me homage, or I'll have him dragged here to Camelot and cut off his beard, and his head as well."

"Well said!" Merlin told Arthur. "But as it begins, so it will go on. There will be many men who try to depose you. But you are the trueborn king of all Britain and must learn to lead your people as your father led them."

After his coronation, King Arthur asked Merlin to tell him the truth about his being trueborn.

"Yes," said Merlin, "you're right to ask, and it is right that you should know."

Then Merlin explained that Queen Ygerna was his mother.

"That's impossible," Arthur said at once.

"No," said Merlin. "It's not impossible."

"But she's Duchess of Cornwall, and she was married to Gorlois, Duke of Cornwall . . ."

"She was."

"And their three daughters are Morgan and her older sisters, Morgause and Elaine."

"That's true as well."

"I'll only believe it . . ." began Arthur, "well, I'll only believe it if Ygerna tells me so herself."

So the following month, soon after the young king had moved to Camelot

with Sir Ector and Sir Kay, Queen Ygerna was escorted there from Tintagel, and with her she brought not only a retinue of ladies but also her beautiful youngest daughter, Morgan, who had caught Arthur's eye and met him in secret some months before.

The magician, accompanied by a large group of knights loyal to Arthur, was there to greet her. The young king himself stood hidden among a group of squires.

"Is what Merlin says true?" Sir Ulfius demanded of Ygerna. "Are you truly Arthur's mother?"

"As Merlin well knows," Queen Ygerna replied, "King Uther came to my bedchamber at Tintagel. Merlin had changed him with magic so that he looked exactly the same as my husband, Gorlois." The queen bowed her head. "In truth, Gorlois was away, guarding Castle Terrible. I didn't know he had been killed only three hours before.

That night I conceived a child, and thirteen days later——as soon as the law of the country allows——King Uther married me. But he'd made a secret agreement with Merlin. I had to give my baby to the magician when he was only two days old. I obeyed, and I never saw him again. I hadn't even had a chance to give him a name." Queen Ygerna's sea-green eyes flooded with tears. "All I know," she said, "is that I bore King Uther's child, believing he was Gorlois's child, and I don't even know who or where he is."

Merlin walked over to the young king and asked him to step forward. Then he led Arthur up to the queen, took Ygerna's right hand and King Arthur's right hand, and linked them.

"Here is your son," he said. "Here is your mother."

Arthur gazed at his mother, and Ygerna gazed at her son.

They gazed, and as when ice first recognizes the warmth of the sun, their thoughts and feelings somehow began to melt, and they were filled with deep longing.

Then the young king embraced his mother and kissed her, and their cheeks streamed with tears.

Sir Ector knelt before them. "Merlin brought your baby safely to my manor," he told the queen.

"Sir Ector and Lady Margery fostered me," Arthur told his mother and the assembly of knights. "They fed me and loved me and taught me. I owe them more, much more, than anyone else in this wide world."

|||||||||||||||||||||||||||||||||||

"My knights keep telling me I should choose a wife," King Arthur told Merlin.

"Quite right," Merlin replied. "You're rising sixteen, aren't you?"

"They keep saying I must have a son and show him at court so that no one doubts who will succeed me."

The magician slowly nodded and stared at Arthur. "But you can't marry Morgan," he said. "I've seen how you're drawn to each other."

"Oh!" exclaimed Arthur, looking startled. "You know, then."

Merlin nodded. "She's your half sister," he said. "I also know that you've made love to her sister Morgause."

Blood reddened Arthur's cheeks. "Without knowing it," he protested. "She gave me a potion to make me think she was Morgan."

"And what you also don't know," the magician went on, "is that Morgause is carrying your child. A baby boy. He will be called Mordred. Arthur, you've committed a terrible sin."

"I was bewitched," said Arthur again.

"Because of this," Merlin went on, "your sister Morgan will grow so jealous that she'll hate you. She'll use her magic powers against any woman you love. Even worse, Mordred, your own son by Morgause, will become your worst enemy. He'll take vengeance on you. But all in good time."

Arthur shielded his ears.

"A wife, eh?" said Merlin, pursing his lips. "A wife . . . Who is it to be, then?"

"I don't know," replied Arthur.

But in his heart of hearts, the young king did know, and Merlin divined it.

Arthur sat very still, looking at his lap and remembering his visit to the court of King Leodegrance when he was only nine——or remembering, rather, the king's only daughter. How spirited she was . . . that light in her eyes . . . and her light voice too, and those little rushes of words . . . how jubilant . . . and her delicious rosebud mouth.

"Guinevere," said Merlin.

Arthur looked up, smiling.

"That's a very bad idea," the magician told him.

"Why a bad idea? A very bad idea. Why, Merlin?"

"Guinevere is just as spirited and as lovely as you think she is. But she'll be faithless, Arthur. She'll be inconsistent."

"No," said Arthur.

"If your heart weren't so set on her, I could find you a wife no less spirited, no less lovely. I'm warning you, Arthur."

"What?"

"Sir Lancelot, the greatest of all your knights, will fall in love with Guinevere, and one day she'll return his love."

"You don't know that," Arthur protested. "You're just saying that, and trying to make me change my mind. I'm decided. I'm going to marry Guinevere."

"You're perverse," said Merlin.

"What does that mean?"

"It means you only accept my advice when it suits you."

When King Leodegrance heard that King Arthur wanted to marry Guinevere, he was elated. "She could make no better marriage," he told his courtiers. "For her dowry, I could offer Arthur estates, but, heaven knows, he has sufficient land already, and Sir Kay will be very hard put to manage them all. But . . . but . . ."

So Leodegrance sent Arthur a gift that King Uther, the young king's own father, had given him many years before when Leodegrance swore lifelong loyalty to him. A table. A massive round table.

A round table that could seat the king's twelve finest knights and King Arthur himself.

Long ago, an ancient chronicler described this table: "It's shaped like half an egg. Like a huge, upside-down beehive. Or like the pale half-moon, lying

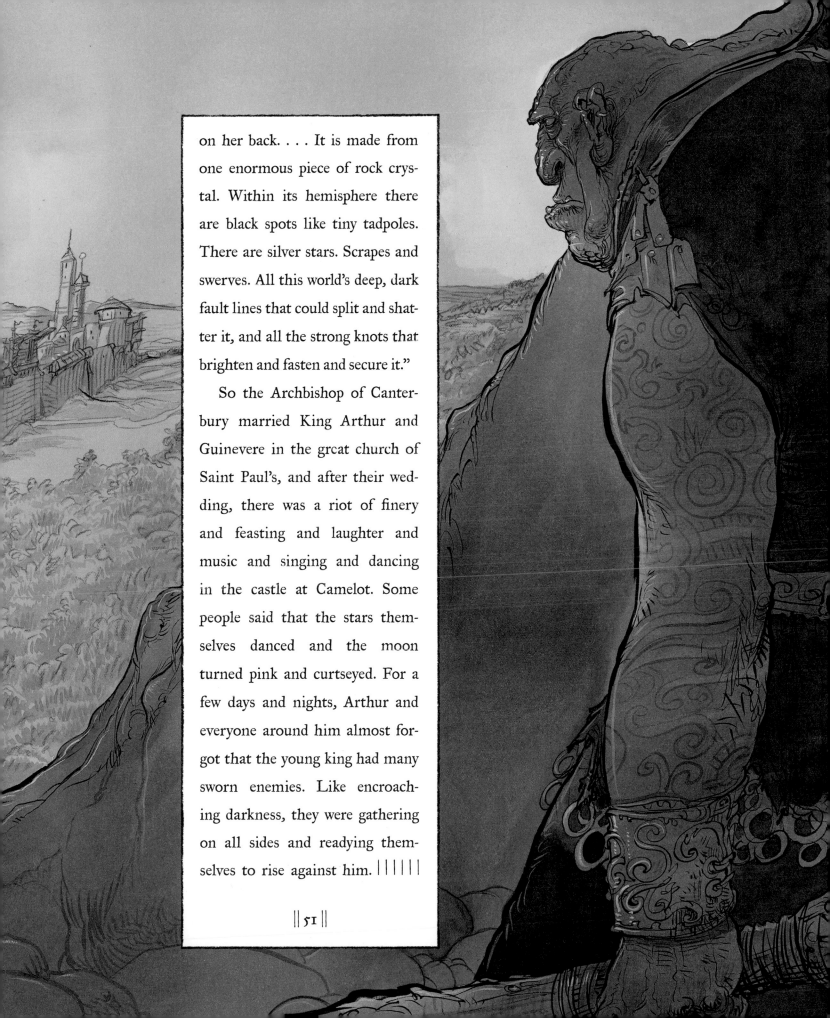

on her back. . . . It is made from one enormous piece of rock crystal. Within its hemisphere there are black spots like tiny tadpoles. There are silver stars. Scrapes and swerves. All this world's deep, dark fault lines that could split and shatter it, and all the strong knots that brighten and fasten and secure it."

So the Archbishop of Canterbury married King Arthur and Guinevere in the great church of Saint Paul's, and after their wedding, there was a riot of finery and feasting and laughter and music and singing and dancing in the castle at Camelot. Some people said that the stars themselves danced and the moon turned pink and curtseyed. For a few days and nights, Arthur and everyone around him almost forgot that the young king had many sworn enemies. Like encroaching darkness, they were gathering on all sides and readying themselves to rise against him. | | | | | |

III

‖ THE FELLOWSHIP OF THE ROUND TABLE ‖

In late April, not long after the wedding celebrations, the young king instructed the overseer at Camelot to install the Round Table in the center of the great hall.

King Leodegrance's men had left it in an outer courtyard after bringing it from Cornwall——first by sea as far as Portsmouth, and then to Camelot on the back of a specially built cart——and it took a dozen brawny men to shoulder it as far as the doors of the great hall. Then they nudged and edged it over the tiled floor. It was so heavy that a number of the pink-and-sepia tiles cracked in half.

King Arthur then told the overseer which knights he had chosen to sit at the Round Table. He had the names of those knights cut into the crystal, and

he commissioned craftsmen to design and make thirteen handsome high-backed chairs of the best elm wood. The thirteenth place at the table was to be left empty.

Secured to the back of each chair was a mounted wooden pole bearing the knight's crested banner and his shield.

To the right of the place reserved for King Arthur was the seat of Sir Lancelot, and to his left Sir Kay, now appointed steward of all the king's lands and estates. To their right and left were Sir Tristram and Sir Lancelot's son, young Sir Galahad, and beyond them, facing each other across the table, sat the brothers Sir Gaheris and Sir Gareth. Farther around sat Sir Gawain, the king's

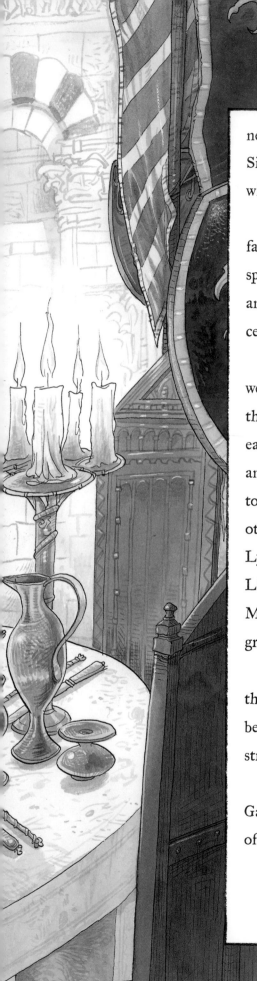

nephew; Sir Geraint; and Sir Lamorak. Sir Lucan and Sir Bedivere were placed with the empty seat between them.

When the table was at last set, it fairly shone with honey candles and sparkled with glasses and silver knives and spoons and spittoons and salt cellars.

Up in the gallery, four trumpeters welcomed the eleven knights into the hall. One by one they strode in, eagerly watched by Queen Guinevere and Lady Lyonesse, who was married to Sir Gareth, as well as a flourish of other ladies——among them Lady Lynette and Lady Laudine and Lady Lionors and Sir Breunor's wife, Lady Maledisant——and, behind them, a great press of squires and servants.

The eleven knights took their seats, then waited for the king. But then they became rather restless and stood up, strutted around, and began to banter.

"If Dagonet had been chosen," Sir Gaheris said, "he'd be playing a couple of spoons by now."

"Dagonet!" exclaimed Sir Gareth.

"What a laugh! He's never even sat on a horse, has he?"

"What about you, Tristram?" said Sir Lamorak. "You're a harpist. Sing us a song."

"Not Tristram!" said Sir Kay. "All he's good for is love songs and laments." And he sniffed and pretended to wipe his eyes.

But then the king strode in. He looked pale, but very calm and determined.

He was younger than any of the knights there, including his own nephew Sir Gawain, the older son of Morgause. He was less than half the age of the oldest, Sir Bedivere, who was thirty-five.

The knights shuffled back to their places, some of them still grinning, and the king looked each one of his Round Table knights in the eye.

"Mark these words!" he told them. "Mark them! I believe each one of you will think back on this day as the greatest day in your life. I believe that long, long after you have died, your descendants will celebrate it."

The king looked up at the gallery and raised his right hand. At once, his trumpeters blew a rousing anthem, while below, in the body of the great hall, Queen Guinevere and her ladies stood up and everyone clapped and cheered. Arthur looked lovingly at his beautiful young queen, and Guinevere returned his gaze.

The king sat down, then spread his arms, inviting his knights to sit as well. Once they were seated, Arthur looked around and asked each of them in turn, "Who are you? What is a knight?"

Some of the knights frowned. Some of the knights looked into the soft glow of the honey candles as if it might illuminate their minds.

"Well, Sir Lancelot?" probed the king.

"A man who has been a squire, sire, and who has then been knighted?" Lancelot tried.

Sir Geraint put up his right hand. "I know. Let me try."

"I hope we all know," said the king with a smile.

"If he's to achieve all he can as a knight," Sir Geraint said, "he'll need the love of a woman. A woman, sire, to support and comfort him."

"Maybe, maybe not," Sir Lancelot said. "I mean, look at Sir Kay! Can you imagine any woman loving him?"

All the knights burst out laughing——all, that is, except Kay.

"His mother loves him!" Arthur gently teased.

All the knights laughed again.

"We can say," Arthur went on, "that knights are fighting men, and fighting men can be like animals. They're fighting men, but don't often have to fight."

"We do, sire," said Sir Galahad. "In tournaments."

"That's pretend fighting," Arthur replied. "I mean, knights don't often fight real battles, and a good thing too. Fighting is very ugly. It makes monsters of men."

"So we knights are men who only play at fighting?" Sir Galahad asked. "You're saying that we are the same as children?"

"No!" said the king, and he raised his voice. "I believe that you will all be upholders."

"Upholders?" Sir Lancelot repeated.

"Imagine a strong, square stone building," Arthur said. "It rests upon a cornerstone and foundation stones. Its massive walls are braced with iron bands. Inside, wide oak beams support the floors and the ceilings . . ."

The knights were nodding, and many were thinking of their own well-fortified homes.

"The stone building is our England," the young king told them. "Our country. And each of you here, and all the lesser knights who serve you, each of you must keep it standing strong."

The young king paused and drank a draft of water.

"Every single day," Arthur went on, "my messengers bring me shocking reports. Horrible reports. Yesterday, I heard of a woman in Shropshire who had been hanged from a tree. Kites had pecked out her eyes and opened her stomach. And in Kent, three men were lying by the wayside, murdered. All higgledy-piggledy. Not even buried. There are horrors everywhere. Everywhere!"

Arthur banged the crystal table with his right fist.

"Without you, my chosen knights, our building, our country, will collapse. And then Emperor Lucius will have no trouble marching in and recapturing our island. It's up to you." The young king leaped to his feet. "It is up to each and every one of you——in your own lands and estates, in your own homes——to uphold justice. Bring robbers and thieves and murderers to book and to court. Put them to good work. Imprison them. Execute them."

King Arthur sat down again and looked around the table, unsmiling. Then he glanced over at his shining young wife, who nodded her agreement and her encouragement.

"What I've seen and learned since I pulled the sword from the stone," the young king said to his knights, "and what Sir Ector and Merlin have taught me, is that any country without a strong king for very long grows weak and falls apart, and it's many months since my father, Uther, died."

Arthur then turned to Sir Lucan. "These knights need wine, don't they? To wash down all these words."

Several of the knights at once assented and rapped the tabletop with their knuckles.

"Ask your cupbearers to come forward," the king told him.

"There's nothing wine will not ease," Sir Gaheris observed.

"And nothing it solves," Sir Bedivere added with a rueful smile.

"Now," said King Arthur, "I must test your patience and ask you a second question."

Several of the knights of the Round Table looked rather glum, and they all prepared themselves by draining their cups of wine.

"You've told me what a knight is," King Arthur began. "So now, my chosen men, what is chivalry? What is chivalry?"

"Ah!" exclaimed Sir Gawain. But that was all he said.

"What about you, Gaheris?" asked the king. "You or your brother."

Sir Gaheris scratched his head. "It's not that I don't know," he began, "but it's difficult to explain."

"When we became squires," Sir Gareth said, "our father, King Lot, said chivalry was several things."

"Being generous," Gaheris said. "With money and gifts."

"Really generous," his brother added. "Not counting exactly how much you give."

"And he said it was not speaking ill of anybody, even if you think poorly of them."

"It's the other way around with me," Sir Kay told him. "I know I'm some-times sharp-tongued——"

"I can vouch for that," King Arthur said, pursing his lips.

"But that doesn't mean I actually think poorly of someone," Kay continued.

"It's being loyal, isn't it?" suggested Sir Bedivere. "Loyal to others, whether you particularly like them or not."

"I think being chivalrous means caring for people who need our help and can't care for themselves," Sir Galahad said. "Orphan children. Wives who've been abandoned or widowed. It means being Christian in thought, word, and deed."

"None of us can be all that," Sir Kay retorted.

"No, but we can mean to be. We can vow to be," Lancelot responded.

"What I think," said Sir Gareth, "or anyhow what I think I think"——several knights laughed and tapped the tabletop——"because discussions like this make me feel rather light-headed . . . is that to be chivalrous, you also have to stay fit. You have to learn how to ride, and hunt, and joust and tourney. Just like when you're a boy, you have to practice your yard skills——running and wrestling and tilting and all that. Yes, you have to be fit to attend to all your duties."

"We can all agree with that," Sir Geraint said, "but isn't that only half of it? What good is it to be fit unless you learn manners, and how to be courteous to ladies? How to serve them? How to love them?"

"That's right," Sir Lancelot and Sir Tristram said together.

"We must try to understand them," Sir Lamorak said, shaking his head, as if there were very little chance of doing so.

"We must understand," Sir Lancelot added, "that women are the same as us, but diffcrent. Many of us marry, and it's better for us if we understand women better before we do! Their bodily strength may not be as great as ours, but their loyalty is often greater."

"And so is the way they comfort and embolden the men they love," Sir Geraint added.

"Provided, that is, that we tell them how we love them," Sir Lancelot said. "Not a few times but many times."

"Their feelings are so strong," Sir Geraint said. "And sometimes so sudden."

"Strange creatures," said Sir Tristram. "Weaker than us, yet stronger than us."

THE SEVEN GREAT TRIALS

FRIENDSHIP
AND BRAVERY

LOVE

HONOR

"Women are rather like chivalry itself then," Sir Gaheris said. "Very difficult to explain!"

"What my foster father, Sir Ector, taught me," King Arthur said, "and what Merlin has taught me, is that chivalry——and I agree with you, it's not easy to explain——chivalry is being noble in your mind and heart. It is thinking and saying the right thing, and knowing that you are. In a way, it's being aware of who you are——each of you. You're knights! So your duty is to serve your king, and to maintain order and justice in your estates. To be responsible . . . to reach out . . . I don't know quite. To care for all the people, the many people whose duty it is to serve you."

All around the table, the knights were nodding in agreement.

"We all have failings," Arthur added. "I know what mine are, all right. But let's try to accept those in one another just as we admire one another's strengths. Let's learn from one another, as I promise to do my best to learn from each of you. We're one family——a family related not by blood but by ideals. And these ideals, they're what I call chivalry."

Again, King Arthur asked Sir Lucan to summon the cupbearers, and then Sir Lucan himself asked, "Sire, why are there twelve of us? I mean, why not seven, or nine, or some number in its prime? Seventeen. Or nineteen."

"If you count that empty seat," the king replied, "there are thirteen places. Another prime number."

Sir Lucan scratched his head. "A baker's dozen," he said, perplexed. "Bad luck? I don't know."

"Like the Apostles?" inquired Sir Bedivere.

"Of course!" King Arthur said.

The knights of the Round Table nodded sagely, those who had already known the answer and those who had not.

"And as you know, the thirteenth place," the king continued, "is the place that belonged to Judas, who betrayed Jesus Christ, then ran away. Isn't that why we believe the number thirteen is unlucky?"

"Ah!" Sir Lucan exclaimed. "I understand."

"And Merlin says," King Arthur added, "that only the most deserving knight of all will be able to sit in it: the knight who achieves the quest for the drinking cup shared by Jesus and his apostles at the Last Supper, the Holy Grail."

"Is that knight one of us?" asked Sir Galahad.

King Arthur shook his head. "I don't know," he said. "I doubt whether even Merlin knows."

For a moment, there was silence. None of the knights wanted to interrupt.

"Again and again, I have had the same dream," King Arthur confided in them. "I've dreamed that in years to come and centuries to come, our Round Table will be remembered as the greatest gathering of knights that ever was. Greater than that at the court of Brutus the Trojan. Greater than the gathering

at the court of the Emperor Alexander. The greatest gathering because it was the most chivalrous. I may not achieve it, and I know that I certainly can't achieve it without each of you."

King Arthur stood up, rather flushed now, and all his knights stood up around him.

"Merlin has told me that this dream can only become true if we succeed in seven great trials. Seven trials!"

"Name them!" the knights called out.

"The first trial is the trial of friendship and bravery. The second is the trial of love, and the third is the trial of honor. The fourth is the trial of magic. The fifth is the quest for the Holy Grail, and the sixth is the trial of love and loyalty. The last trial is the trial of the blood knot."

All the knights at the table and everyone in the great hall stood absolutely silent, spellbound, listening to the young king.

"Seven steps!" King Arthur called out. "Seven trials. You and I and all of us, we'll face them together." | | | |

MAGIC

THE QUEST FOR THE
HOLY GRAIL

LOVE AND
LOYALTY

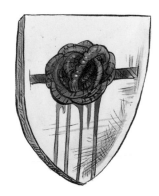

THE **BLOOD KNOT**

IV

‖ THE TRIAL OF FRIENDSHIP AND BRAVERY ‖

Sir Bedivere and the Giant

From the start, it was the young king's wish to ride south and west in early September with his wife and household, and to stay at his castle at Caerleon on the borders of Wales. There the king held court, and many of his knights went hunting and jousted in the ruins of the old Roman amphitheater.

But then the Emperor Lucius sent the young king a rude message from Rome, reminding him that all of Britain had once been part of the Roman Empire, and so also accusing him of failing to pay the annual tribute due to Rome, and threatening to invade.

The king convened a council of his leading earls and barons and knights, and they were angry and outspoken and at once decided to resist Lucius.

So the king instructed Lucius' messengers to take back this threatening message to the emperor:

"King Arthur has not the least intention of paying you as much as one pound of tribute, and he is gathering a huge army and will very soon be on his way to attack Rome."

"I thirst for the blood of my enemies," Sir Lamorak declared, "and it's as if I'd felt thirsty for three whole days and not allowed to drink a sip of spring water."

‖ 64 ‖

Then the king and his retinue hurried back to Camelot, where he signed an order that as the law of the land decreed, his young wife, Guinevere, should act as his regent and rule the kingdom during his absence, and should care for his little son, Mordred.

||||||||||||||||||||||||||||||||||

"This is your first trial," Merlin told the king. "It's a trial of the fellowship of your huge army, of knights and commoners who come from many different countries. But it's also a demanding, dangerous trial of friendship between two men."

"As for that," said Arthur. "Well, I'll take Kay. I've known him since before I can remember."

Merlin frowned and gently shook his head. "No, no," he said.

"Then Sir Dagonet! He'll make me laugh, even when there's terrible danger."

The corners of Merlin's eyes crinkled. "Laughter is all very well, but your companion must be tempered . . . tempered like a fine sword."

"Yes," said Arthur. "Sir Bedivere,  then. He's the most seasoned and trustworthy of all my knights."

"A good choice," Merlin agreed.

"We must leave at once."

"Arthur, Arthur, you're always in such a hurry. The Emperor Lucius is extremely powerful. He's threatening to invade and recapture Britain. Look at you! You haven't even got a sword. You must learn patience, or you'll defeat yourself."

"I have a sword!" protested Arthur.

Merlin shook his head. "The sword you pulled from the stone is a sword for ceremonies. You must have your own battle sword as well."

Arthur and Merlin cantered out of Camelot on the same dear riding horses they had brought up to London from Sir Ector's manor.

"Your mount looks rather thin, Merlin," Arthur observed. "And so do you."

Merlin gave a faint smile. "We keep in step," he said.

The sky was ribbed with high, white clouds, and what wind there was came from the south, little more than a waft of mild September air. For the most part, Arthur and Merlin rode side by side, talking about the old horse breeds——Andalusian and Arabian and Turkoman and the like. But then Merlin rode some way ahead, and while he was in the middle of a wood, three youths came galloping at him through the trees, yelling. At once, they began to lay into him with their cudgels.

"Snouts!" shouted Merlin. "Snouts!"

Arthur saw what was happening and spurred his horse. As soon as the youths saw that Arthur was fully armed, they wheeled around and rode back into the woods.

"Merlin!" cried Arthur. "You could've been killed."

"No!" Merlin replied. "They were just snouts. I could have saved myself if I'd wanted to."

"Snouts?"

"Youths on the lookout for horses. Spies for armed men." Merlin gave his left shoulder a rub. "No," he said again and then, more quietly, "you're nearer to your death day than I am to mine."

But Arthur didn't hear him.

In mid-afternoon, the two of them came to a lake. An old boat was lying at the water's edge.

"This is where you'll find your battle sword," Merlin announced.

The water was still. Almost glassy. It told the drifting clouds and flying birds their own stories.

But then, out in the middle of the lake, the water became disturbed. It began to shudder.

And while Arthur and Merlin stood by the boat and watched, a sword rose out of the water, and then a hand holding the sword and an arm wrapped in rich white silk.

"There is your sword!" the magician exclaimed.

A young woman came walking over the water toward them.

"The Lady of the Lake," Merlin said.

"That sword," the young woman said to Arthur, "you may have it, if you agree to give me whatever I ask for."

"Whatever you ask for . . . All right! I will."

"At the right time, I will ask you for what I need," the young woman informed him. "But for now, row out with your companion. Take the sword and its scabbard from the hand."

Arthur and Merlin secured their palfreys to two oak trees. Then Merlin manned the oars of the old boat at the water's edge. When they approached the hand and the arm wrapped in rich white silk, Arthur reached out and grasped the sword by its cross guards.

Carefully, the young king drew the sword from its scabbard. He examined it. He waved it. He examined it again. He laughed for sheer happiness.

"Which do you prefer?" asked Merlin. "The sword or the scabbard?"

"The sword of course. You can't fight with a scabbard."

"Things are not always what they seem," the magician said. "This scabbard is worth ten swords. Arthur, be sure to wear it wherever you go. Absolutely sure! For as long as you're wearing it, you'll never shed a drop of blood, no matter how badly you're wounded."

Arthur turned the gleaming sword and its scabbard over and over in his hands.

"The sword is called Excalibur," Merlin told him.

||||||||||||||||||||||||||||||||||||

From all over the country, columns and clusters of men and horses, all of them supporters of King Arthur, converged on the south coast of England and set sail from Southampton for the little port of Barfleur, in Normandy. There they pitched camp and awaited the arrival of their allies——the armies of the kings of Norway and Denmark, and of the islands of Ireland and Iceland, Gotland and Orkney.

How many men assembled there? It wasn't easy to count them, let alone feed them, and they raided the farms for miles and miles around. One hundred and fifty thousand, some people said. Even more, said others.

It was only a few days before messengers from the Emperor Lucius galloped into King Arthur's camp. The emperor, they told him, was rounding up a huge army of men from Greece and Syria and Spain and Africa——an army of four hundred and sixty thousand men—— and it would only be a matter of days before they reached Normandy.

"Sufficient unto the day," said Merlin.

"What does that mean?" asked Arthur.

"Didn't Sir Ector teach you? 'Take no thought for tomorrow: tomorrow will look after itself.' Today's evil is quite bad enough as it is."

"What evil?" asked Arthur.

The magician ballooned his cloak, and when he stood on his toes, Arthur could hear some of them cracking.

"A giant!" boomed Merlin. "A giant of a giant has stumped up here all the way from Spain. He's no respecter of kings or emperors. He makes his own rules."

Then Arthur's brother, Sir Kay, lifted the flap of the king's tent and entered.

"Kay!" Arthur exclaimed. "Have you heard about the giant?"

"A giant of a giant!" Merlin added. "He's snatched Helena, the niece of Duke Hoel, and carried her up to the top of Mont-Saint-Michel."

"I'll win her back," said Arthur hotly.

The magician smiled a thin, grim smile. "The duke's men tried to land there, but Mont-Saint-Michel rises straight out of the sea. The giant hurled down boulders and sank their boats. When the men tried to climb up to attack him, the giant captured and ate seven of them."

"This is surely our first trial," the young king said. "I'll take Sir Bedivere with me. And you, Kay. Will you come too?"

"I will," said Arthur's brother.

"The giant's worse than a griffin," Merlin warned them. "Worse than the hyenas who devour the bodies of dead women."

"If I can kill him," the young king said, "the victory will inspire my whole army. Even outnumbered, we could defeat Lucius."

That night, Arthur lay on his camp bed, surrounded by a sea of tents and sleeping men. From time to time, he heard dogs barking, and then a far horn sounded . . .

Maybe he drowsed a little, but what with snatches of memory and moments of anxiety, Arthur didn't sleep. So at two o'clock in the morning, he got up, dressed, and roused Kay and Sir Bedivere in their tents.

The three rode out of the camp, followed by their squires. Within an hour, they reached the little harbor and beach across from the twin summits of the Mount, each with a fire blazing on top of it.

"Row over in advance of us to scout things out," Arthur told Sir Bedivere, "then report back."

Several small boats used by local people for fishing and crossing between the mainland and the Mount were lying side by side on the beach. Arthur and Kay shouldered one and carried it down to the sleeping water. Then one-armed Sir Bedivere clambered in and grasped an oar and tucked the other into his

left armpit. He dipped his oars so quietly, and raised them so cautiously, that one could barely hear the salty drops drip-dropping from them.

Soon after he had reached the little stone landing and begun to scramble up toward the lower of the two fires, sometimes on his feet, sometimes using his arm, the silken night was ripped apart by a scream.

Sir Bedivere halted but heard nothing further. It was as if the warm night were still sleeping and the scream had been only inside his own head.

Bedivere used his dagger to help pull himself up the Mount's rocky face. But when he reached the top, there was nothing there, nothing to see but the fire, spitting and burning merrily.

Sir Bedivere screwed up his eyes and peered into the darkness. At last, he thought he could make out a shape. A lump. A kind of earth mound, was it?

Treading very lightly, he approached it and found an old woman, slumped and weeping, hopelessly weeping.

The knight knelt before her and took the old woman's stringy hands between his own one hand.

The old woman shivered, and what teeth she had chattered. Her whole body shook.

"Trust me," said Sir Bedivere. "Tell me what has happened."

"I was her nurse," the old woman said in a low, cracked voice, a voice that might once have been beautiful. "She was my second self. Helena. When the giant snatched her up and squeezed her in his arms, she was so terrified, her heart stopped beating. So the monster threw her away like a rag. My soul sister . . . Helena." The old woman's breath became more and more jerky. "The giant seized me instead and abused me. I swear by God, I swear by all the years of my life."

"Be calm now," Sir Bedivere told her. "Be calm."

"With my own hands, I've just buried her. Helena, my second self. Here in this mound," the old woman told him. She sobbed and screwed up her eyes.

"Are you mad?" she demanded. "What are you doing here? When he comes back and finds you . . ."

For some while, the knight sat in silence beside the distraught old woman, and then he said, "I could never fight this giant on my own, with one arm, but

one of my companions is a young man as loyal to me as I am to him."

Then Sir Bedivere stood up. "I'll return as soon as I can," he told her. "I promise you." Then he strode away, virtually cascaded down the Mount in a shower of grit and pebbles, and rowed across to the beach.

When they heard what had happened, the two brothers were appalled.

Arthur spat on the sand. "Filth! Hideous!" he exclaimed. "I'll fight this giant. I'll fight him alone."

"Impossible!" exclaimed Sir Bedivere.

The three men rowed back across to the Mount and, standing on the little stone landing there, Arthur repeated, "I'll fight him alone. I'll go on ahead, but if you hear me calling out for you, come up as fast as you can."

Sir Bedivere lowered his head and somehow nodded and shook it at the same time.

As the young king climbed toward the higher of the two fires, the whole of the eastern sky was turning rose pink and misty. The sun was just about to rise. Very soon after it did so, two sun dogs appeared, shining and flaring on either side of it.

It's an omen, thought Arthur. It must be. But is it good or bad? Merlin would know.

The giant's face was coated with dried blood. His eyelashes and eyebrows were matted with fat from the leg of pork he was gnawing while three more sucklings roasted on their spits over the embers.

The moment he saw his visitor, he dived for his huge oak club, and although Arthur drew Excalibur, raised his shield, and rushed at him, the giant was too agile. He scooped up his club and slammed the young king's shield. Arthur was deafened, and the waves swilling around the bottom of the Mount kicked up in shock.

Then Arthur aimed high. He lunged, and with Excalibur, he gashed the giant's forehead. Blood poured down his face; it flooded his eyes and blinded him.

The giant bellowed and rushed at Arthur; he grabbed him around his waist and forced him onto his knees. But the young king ducked right down, slipped out of the giant's deadly grasp, and leaped to his feet.

Gasping, Arthur struck at the giant again and again. He carved the giant's right shoulder; he shattered his left elbow; he sliced off both his kneecaps and unbraced his right hip, giving him no time to recover from one blow before the next.

No time! No time at all! Then Arthur dealt the giant his death blow! He drove the whole length of Excalibur through his right ear and up into his brain.

The hideous giant howled. He stumbled sideways; he tottered and fell.

The young king yelled for Sir Bedivere and his brother. But although he didn't know it, they had been following close behind him, and as soon as they heard the appalling howl, they scrambled up the slope.

Then they saw.

They saw Arthur hoisting his shield to heaven and the giant lying dead at his

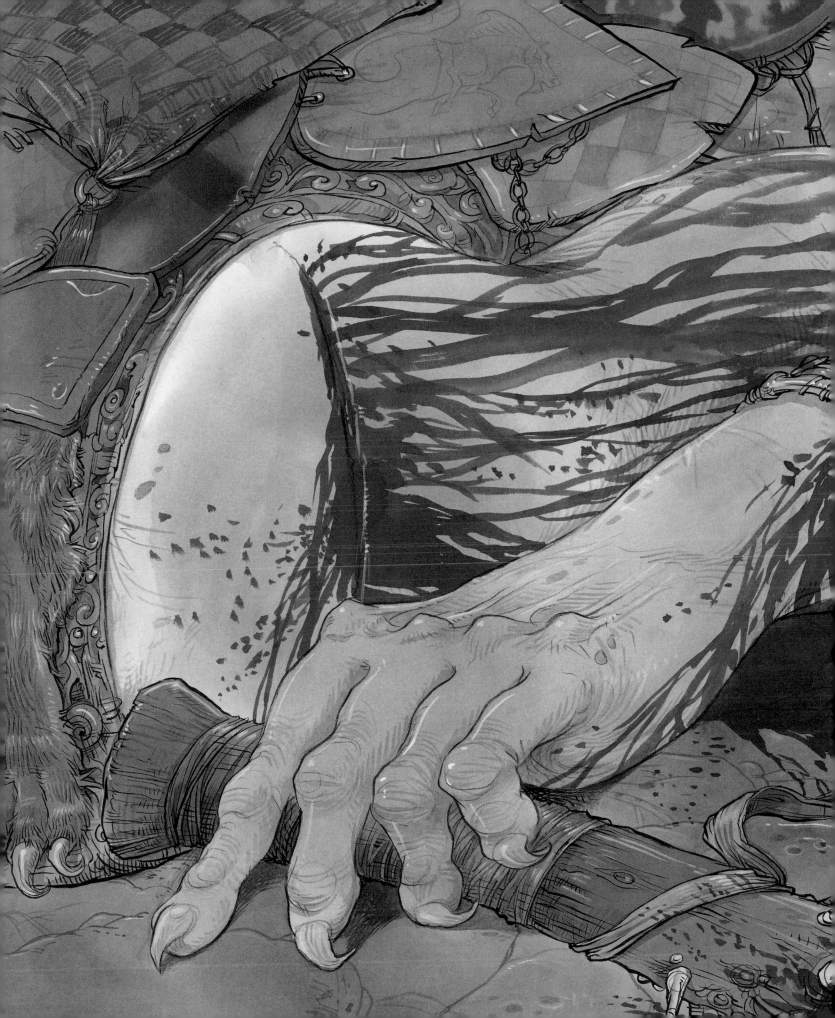

feet. They cheered hoarsely and raised their own shields.

"Hack off his head," Arthur instructed them. "Tell your squires to come and carry it back to our camp."

Sir Bedivere gazed at the young king. Then he got down on one knee, but Arthur at once took his arm and raised him. "I'll go down to the old woman," the young king panted. "I'll tell her the giant is dead and lead her to safety."

Few of the hundreds of knights assembled in the camp were even aware that Arthur and his two companions had ridden out in the middle of the night. News of their return, however, and of their grisly trophy, spread like wildfire. The giant's head was stuck to a pike, and crowds of men gathered around and gaped at it.

Duke Hoel, alas, grieved at the death of his niece Helena. He vowed to build a chapel in her name on top of the Mount.

"Without you," Arthur told Sir Bedivere, "I could never have killed the giant. You scouted for me. And what you told me about Helena and the

old woman made my blood boil and emboldened me."

"I'm far from fearless," Sir Bedivere replied. "Were it not for you, I'd never have dared climb the Mount. I will serve you now and always."

The young king and his knight embraced, and Arthur turned to his brother, Kay. "I know how loyal you are," he said quietly, "and how loyal you always will be. Kay, your loyalty is part of my strength."

Kay smiled a wry smile. "And I know how brave you are," he replied, "but when you told me you were going to fight the giant alone, I thought you'd very likely be leaving us all without a leader."

Then King Arthur addressed as many men as could hear him. "It may seem strange," he called out, "to hear me say we can defeat Lucius's army merely because I've succeeded in killing the giant of Mont-Saint-Michel. Lucius has three times as many men as we do, after all. But that's what I believe. Success leads to confidence. Confidence leads to victory. That's the truth of it."

King Arthur and his army surged through France. They won one battle after another against the armies of the Roman Emperor. But as they were about to march south over the Alps into Italy and launch an attack on Rome herself, some of Arthur's knights started to squabble about food supplies. First they brawled, and then they skirmished. Several men were killed.

Soon after this, messengers arrived from Britain, Merlin among them, bearing news that some of the older knights who had stayed at home were unhappy with Guinevere's headstrong decisions and poor judgment. They believed her to be too young and inexperienced and had even begun to talk about deposing her.

To win Rome but lose my own country, Arthur thought. Where's the sense in that?

"Nowhere," said Merlin, smiling at Arthur. "Nowhere."

"So I have no choice," Arthur said. "We must turn for home."

"At once," Merlin agreed.

Many young men had shown outstanding bravery, unflinching loyalty, and selfless friendship during the battles against Lucius's allies: Sir Lancelot; his younger brother, Sir Lionel; the French knight Sir Yvain; Sir Cador of Cornwall; and the king's nephew Sir Gawain. King Arthur rewarded each of them with gold spurs.

"I remember that you told me I'd need more places at the Round Table," Arthur said to Merlin, "and I can see now that I will."

"Not yet," the magician replied. "You can reward a man without immediately admitting him to the Round Table."

"But they've proven themselves. They're eager and impatient——"

"Not as impatient as you are!" Merlin said. "True, you've undergone the trial of friendship and bravery, the first of the seven stages of knighthood. But before long, you and your knights must face the second trial." ||||||

V

|| THE TRIAL OF LOVE ||

SIR GERAINT AND ENID

"Arthur!" whispered Guinevere, her whole body trembling.

"What a fine husband I've been!" said Arthur ruefully. "We've been married five years, but I've been away in France for four of them."

They gazed into each other's eyes for a long thirsty moment, then wrapped their arms around each other. Their hearts were so highly strung that they thought they might burst or snap.

And because there was so much they had dreamed of saying to each other, they were scarcely able to say anything at all.

How long did they embrace?

As far as it is from memory to imagination.

King Arthur then greeted his son, Mordred, heir to the throne.

That is to say, he picked him up as if he were thistledown and tossed him into the air and caught him, laughing, and then tossed him up again.

Mordred was not amused. "Put me down!" he said angrily.

"You're six," exclaimed Arthur. "Six, Mordred! When I was six, I remember going cliff-fishing with my brother, Kay. I'd better watch out or you'll catch up with me."

For a few days, the castle of Camelot felt foreign to Arthur. But in time it grew familiar, again, and as if he'd scarcely been away at all. Familiar and very dear.

Before long, though, the Roman Emperor Lucius sent messengers to tell the king that winning a few battles wasn't the same as winning a war. He threatened to invade Britain before the end of the year.

"You are insolent and you are stupid!" was the emperor's message to King Arthur. "You are very young and very green. Do you really believe Britain is free to decide whether or not to belong to the empire? It is not. I will reclaim the whole island and punish you severely for your arrogance."

But the young king and the knights of the Round Table figured that Lucius was too weakened to carry out his threats anytime soon. More pressing were the bitter complaints some of the elder knights had lodged against Guinevere: weak leadership and poor decisions during his absence. He summoned the disgruntled knights, one by one, to court and listened to their grievances. Then he entreated each of them to make peace with his young wife.

On their way to the castle at Caerleon,

in the Welsh Marches, where Arthur always held court at Whitsun, the young king and Merlin had a conversation.

"There are still so many disputes," Arthur said. "So much hatred. Robberies and murders. Men behaving like animals. Packs of wolves! Pig-headed donkeys! Things are worse than they were before I left for France."

"You must resolve them one by one," Merlin replied, "and keep reminding the knights of your Round Table to support you and to address injustice on their own estates and whenever they ride out."

Their horses plodded dolefully through the rain.

"Remember: you were born to lead," Merlin said. "Trueborn. It's not easy, I know." The magician hesitated. "And I won't always be here to help you."

Arthur turned in his saddle to face Merlin. "Why? Where will you be?"

"Where will I be? Well, I don't suppose for one moment that I'll be stranded at midnight on the top of Cader Idris, either turning mad or becoming a poet."

"Which would be worse?" asked Arthur.

"You mean between being a mad poet or a poetic madman? Is there much difference?"

Arthur laughed.

"And I don't suppose my sister——"

"What sister?" exclaimed Arthur. "I didn't know you had a sister."

"She's called Ganieda," Merlin said. "Sometimes I scarcely remember myself that I have a sister. Anyhow, I doubt she'll be building me an observatory where I can sit through the centuries, observing the stars."

"Where will you be?" Arthur repeated.

"I can tell you only what I've already told my own apprentice, the bewitching young Nimue. She doesn't yet have the powers your own sister Morgan has, but she's learning fast."

"She is!" agreed Arthur. "Her eyes! She could work loose an arrow in your shoulder simply by staring at it or draw a deep splinter out of your hand by glancing at it!"

"And she can wrestle words out of me against my will," added the magician. "As I've told Nimue, one day I'll go away and take with me the treasures of Britain——the sword that bursts into flame, the scarlet gown, and the whetstone, the golden chessboard——yes, I'll take all thirteen of them and keep them safe until you wake and come back."

"Wake?" asked Arthur. "Come back? What do you mean?"

Merlin simply shook his head and pulled up his hood.

That night, the two of them sheltered under a dripping tree.

Within two minutes, Merlin was sleeping like a baby.

What a very strange man he is, thought Arthur. Sometimes he riles me and only answers my questions with questions. He certainly doesn't always tell me what I want to hear, but I can't imagine being without him.

||||||||||||||||||||||||||||||||||||||

After King Arthur and his court celebrated Whitsun at the end of May, some of his knights rode out armed only with

crossbows and quivers of arrows, to hunt for the White Stag.

Ahead of them ran the beaters. Around them, their hounds barked and yelped. And behind them followed Queen Guinevere, accompanied by Olwen, one of her young ladies-in-waiting.

Quail and grouse and partridge flapped out of the forest as fast as they could. Rabbits disappeared down their holes. Hares and foxes stayed low, very low. Wild boar lay still as stones. And somewhere, the White Stag waited.

One knight, Sir Geraint, had overslept! Like Guinevere, he came from the west country. They had known each other since they were children because their fathers were neighbors and good friends.

Geraint woke up with a start! The sun was already climbing, and reproaching him through his small window.

He pulled on his clothes without waiting for his squire to dress him, and what clothes they were! A silk coat from Constantinople embroidered with hundreds of little flowers. Dark-green brocade leggings. An ermine mantle.

As Sir Geraint galloped into the forest on his courser, he could hear the sounds of the hunt: the hallooing, the barking of the hounds, the hunting horns, sometimes excited, sometimes strangely melancholy.

Hou! Hou! they blared. *Hou! Hou!* and then *Hoouuu! Hoouuu!*

Sir Geraint caught up with the queen and Olwen.

"Greetings!" he called out. "I'm late, late, late! And do you know why? So I could have the pleasure of your company."

Guinevere laughed. "Is that so? Not because you overslept?"

"No, no!"

"I've heard what your father calls you. 'Sleepyhead! A Devon slugabed!'"

So the queen's and Sir Geraint's horses fell into step, but somehow they lost track of the hunt, rather as a pack of hounds can quite suddenly lose the scent of a fox. And when they paused in a lumi-

nous green glade, they could hear nothing but their horses gasping and snorting, and their own heavy breathing.

Then out of a stand of beech trees in front of them ambled a knight armed with a shield and lance, and a maiden, both riding warhorses. Leading the knight and maiden was a dwarf astride a shambling nag. The dwarf was wielding a scourge——a hard, knotted rope.

"Olwen," said the queen, "please ask that knight to present himself to me, and to bring the maiden with him."

"Stand back!" the dwarf warned, his voice like a fretsaw. "You've no business approaching anyone as fine as my master."

"But my lady, the queen——" Olwen began.

"I'm warning you," croaked the dwarf. And then he raised his scourge again and lashed her across the back of her right hand.

Guinevere was outraged. "The monster! Geraint, ride over to that arrogant knight and tell him to come over here at once."

"Stand back!" the dwarf snapped. "I'm warning you."

Sir Geraint and his courser tried to

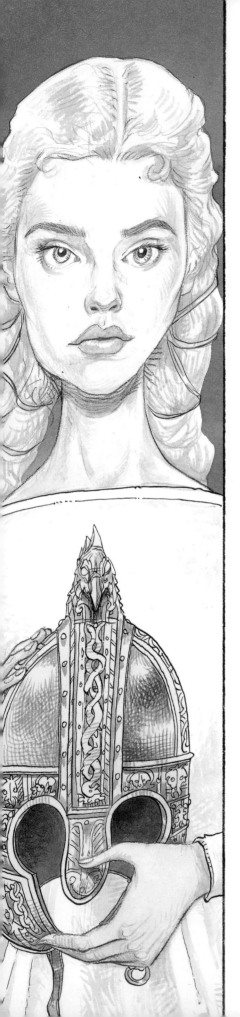

push the dwarf and his nag out of the way, but the dwarf only scowled and lashed the knight across the forehead, nose, and neck.

Geraint's face was striped with bloody gashes.

"My face is cut to ribbons," he said to the queen.

"It is."

"My lady, armed or not, I'm going to follow him."

"You don't have to prove your bravery to me," the queen told him.

"I have to prove it to myself," replied Geraint.

"God go with you, then," said the queen. "God save you from harm, Geraint."

Sir Geraint followed the knight, the maiden, and the dwarf back through the forest to a castle belonging to a count and saw the knight dismount and enter it. Geraint rode on down a rough track until he came to a little cottage. It belonged to a poor man.

"I wasn't always this poor," the man told Geraint. "But I've been caught up in conflicts and drowning in debts, and I lost almost everything."

"Do you know where I can borrow a set of armor?" Sir Geraint asked him. "New or old, it doesn't matter."

The man led him to a back room, and when Sir Geraint clapped eyes on all the armor there, he hadn't the least doubt that the poor man had indeed once been rich and powerful.

"You can borrow whatever you like," the man told him.

Now the old man and his wife had a daughter. Though she was clad in a homespun dress, worn through at the elbows, she was nevertheless lovely. Sir Geraint began to talk with her and noticed how still she sat and how quiet and courteous she was. When he watched the expert way in which she cared for his courser, when they spoke by the fireside until after midnight and when she looked at him so steadily with shining eyes, when she lovingly armed him herself the next morning, limb by limb, his heart began to thump and double-thump!

The next morning, crowds gathered outside the castle to watch the annual contest for a fine sparrow hawk, chained to a silver perch.

Sir Geraint challenged the arrogant knight for it, something no knight had dared to do for the past three years.

"Be off!" the knight told him. "No one can withstand me."

Nevertheless, they jousted, and Sir Geraint unseated the knight and threw him to the ground. Then he dispatched him to Caerleon to beg for the queen's mercy for the way his dwarf had lashed Guinevere's young attendant, Olwen.

That evening, Geraint revealed his identity to the poor man and his wife.

"I'm the son of King Lac," he said.

"Ah! We've often heard about you," the old man said. "About your courage and your loyalty."

Then Sir Geraint boldly asked the man for his daughter's hand, and the girl's face shone.

"With my daughter here beside me," the poor man said, "I've never cared as much as a

marble for the riches of the whole world. You'll take her away, I know, but I'm willing for her to be betrothed to you."

And then the girl's mother and her father wept bittersweet tears.

"I know I sometimes talk too much," Geraint told the girl, "and you say so little."

"I reply when I've got reason to," she told him with a shy smile. "I know how to look after myself."

When Sir Geraint and his sweetheart reached Caerleon, they made their way straight to Queen Guinevere. Geraint told the queen that poor as she looked, dressed in nothing but a simple white smock, the girl was not only nobly born but also skilled and courteous and had a mind of her own.

"You can see for yourself!" exclaimed Sir Geraint. "You can see how she shines! I'm intent on marrying her."

"So soon?" said Guinevere, arching her eyebrows and smiling.

"Intent!" exclaimed Sir Geraint.

"My dear friend!" said the queen. "My all-or-nothing knight!"

|| 90 ||

Then Guinevere took the girl away to her own chambers, and there her ladies-in-waiting tried different dresses on her. They all settled on the very dress the girl had tried on first and liked best: a silk mantle that had a way of looking purple in the one light and dark green in another and was embroidered with dozens, in fact with hundreds, of little white crosses.

Then his sweetheart told Geraint her true name, as a sign that she was ready to marry him.

"Enid," she said. "Enid is the name with which I was christened."

"How fitting," Geraint said. "Your name tells who you are: spotless and pure." After the Archbishop of Canterbury pronounced them man and wife and Enid vowed to love, honor, and obey her husband——oh! the sheer delight, the happiness at court. Acrobats and conjurors and fire-eaters performed in the great hall. There was dancing and storytelling and singing. Every few minutes, another band struck up——fiddlers, flautists,

pipers, trumpeters, players of timbrels and tabors and flageolets.

All this to say nothing about the variety of meat and fish and wine, or how the king pulled out Mordred's first wobbly tooth, or how Sir Kay drank too much and went around the hall with a sour mouth, or how Sir Dagonet tried to juggle and dropped a whole pile of plates. King Arthur opened the gates of his castle to everyone, and his bakers and cooks and cupbearers gave them all, rich and poor, just as much food and drink as they desired.

Then the king held a tournament, and many of the counts and earls and knights who had come to Caerleon to celebrate the wedding took part in it. Geraint wore Enid's love token and fought like a man possessed. No one could match him except the king's own nephew Sir Gawain. But after rounds of jousting and tilting and swordplay, even Gawain had to yield, and Sir Geraint was declared victor of the tournament.

"Everything ends, alas," Sir Geraint said. "Even these glorious days. I must now take Enid to Carnant, my own lands."

"I'll miss you," the king said, "and so will Guinevere."

Sir Geraint smiled and bowed his head. "What matters more than dear friends?" he asked.

Merlin stood beside Arthur on the battlements, and they watched until Sir Geraint and Lady Enid and their small retinue were lost in a white mist.

"He's so headstrong," observed Arthur.

The magician smiled a little smile. "And you're not?"

"No!" said Arthur. "Well, he's so headstrong and so headlong. Guinevere calls him her all-or-nothing knight."

||||||||||||||||||||||||||||||||||||

Three months had slipped away, the best of summer come and gone. As day dawned, Geraint and Enid lay in bed facing each other.

Geraint was asleep. Enid was not.

Then Enid began to sniffle and to sigh.

He's done nothing at all since the day we arrived here, she thought. *He's been a knight in name only, not in deed and truth. He's ignored all his duties.*

Enid sniffled again.

"It's all my fault," she whispered to herself. "It's because of me. I've snared him."

Then Enid gave a loud sob, and that woke Geraint up.

"My sweetheart!" he exclaimed. "What's wrong?"

Enid burst into tears and clutched her husband. "It's all my fault. I've brought shame on you."

"Shame? What do you mean? You're my wife, my lover, my mistress, my sweetheart. No one and nothing matters to me except you."

"Everyone is talking behind your back," Enid told him. "Your friends. The knights here at your father's court. Your servants."

Geraint sat up. "Why? What are they saying?"

"That you've forgotten you're a knight. They ask what you've done of late to help the helpless. Or to right some wrong. You haven't even contested a tournament. They're saying it's all because you're infatuated with me." Then Enid began to sob again. "You of all men! They're mocking you."

Geraint squared his shoulders and gritted his teeth. "Right!" he said. "Get up! Go and put on your best gown. Have the grooms saddle your best northern palfrey."

Now Enid looked scared. "Are you . . . ? Are you sending me away?"

Geraint turned his back on his wife and strode to his own dressing room. There his squire dressed and armed him: gauntlets of shining steel, a rust-proof coat of mail so well woven that you couldn't pass a needle between the links, and a helmet girdled by a broad gold band.

Then he told his squire to hurry down to the stables and tell the grooms to saddle to his wonderful Gascon bay.

"Stop at my wife's dressing room. Tell her I'm waiting. Ask her what's keeping her so long."

By the time Geraint and Enid met in the castle courtyard, most of King Lac's household had assembled, surprised and very pleased to see Sir Geraint fully armed again. Many of his knights and squires were there too, eager to accompany him.

"No, no!" Sir Geraint cried. "I need no companions, none at all except for my wife."

Once the knight and his wife had ridden through the portcullis, Geraint pulled up his bay. "Now," he instructed Enid, "you're not to speak to me. Not one word!"

"Not speak to you?"

"You heard me. Even if you see I'm in danger, you're not to speak a word. Ride on ahead of me, and keep a steady pace."

Is he testing me? Enid wondered. Testing himself? It's very dangerous to travel on our own.

How right Enid was.

Within a couple of hours, they were spotted by three robber-knights. When they saw Lady Enid with Sir Geraint well behind her, they could scarcely believe their eyes.

"What a beauty!" exclaimed the first man.

"The lady?" said the second.

"No! Her palfrey! Look at her. So eager, so high-stepping. The horse is all I want."

"I'm going to ride around behind the knight," the second man said. "I'll attack him from behind."

"And I'll take him head-on," said the third. "Together, we'll hack him down."

As soon as Lady Enid spied the robbers approaching, she turned around in her saddle and called out. "Husband! Husband! Watch out!"

"What!" Sir Geraint bawled, outraged at Enid's call, then wheeled around and drove his lance straight through the second robber's chest.

At once, the third robber attacked Geraint and each struck the other's shield. But the robber-knight's lance splintered, and with his second thrust, Geraint wounded him in the chest and unseated him.

Then the robber who coveted Enid's palfrey hurried away into the forest, but Sir Geraint pursued him and with one whack, toppled him from his saddle.

Geraint rounded up the robber-knights' horses——three handsome coursers, one milky white, one black and glossy, the third almost as dappled as Enid's northern palfrey.

"I warned you not to say a word," he said to his wife. "I don't want to have to warn you again."

Lady Enid bowed her head.

"Even if you see I'm in danger, not a word unless I say you may speak."

Is he testing me? Enid wondered again. Testing himself? Proving himself to me?

On they rode until they came to a group of battered old oaks, where five mounted men were lying in wait.

She couldn't help herself. Enid turned around in her saddle and called, "Husband! Geraint!"

"Again?" he bellowed. "You don't have the slightest regard for me or what I say."

Then four of the men attacked him while the fifth grabbed Enid and tried to pull her out of her saddle.

But the five men fared no better than the three robber-knights before them. Geraint planted the tip of his lance into the neck of one man just below his chin, and his throat flowered with scarlet blood; one man's horse fell on top of him and lay there for so long that the man drowned in a shallow pool; one lost his head; one's collarbone was broken. The fifth man broke away from Enid and threw down his lance. Then he abandoned his horse and Geraint left him cowering behind the trunk of one of the old oaks.

Sir Geraint and Enid rounded up all five extra horses and rode on. But they couldn't find anywhere at all to shelter for the night.

"We'll get what cover we can under this laburnum," Geraint told his wife.

Enid meekly nodded.

"I'll watch over you," Geraint told her.

"No," replied Enid. "You're the weary one. You've fought tooth and nail."

This time, Geraint didn't reprove Enid for speaking to him, and he didn't object. He lay down, and Enid spread her lilac silk gown over him. All that September night, she kept watch, and all night, she held the reins of the eight horses.

"I'll obey you, yes," she said to herself, "but I'll make you need me, even if you don't realize you do."

The laburnum shivered; poor Enid shivered. When she looked up at the stars, almost white and heartless, she saw that they were shivering too.

On Geraint and Enid rode, early, very early, stiff in their saddles, hoping to find someone who could offer them something to eat and drink.

They came into a valley, with the eight horses they had captured

in tow——all of them restless and agitated because they were hungry and thirsty too. It was almost midday before they saw anyone at all.

"Men! I can fight men," Sir Geraint grumbled. "But rumbling hunger! Sharp thirst! They're worse enemies."

At last they rode up behind three young men: a squire with two lads. They were carrying flagons of wine and flour-cakes and wedges of goat's cheese for the haymakers farther up the valley.

"We've come down from my master's castle," the squire told them. "The Count of Limors. Can you see it? Up there, guarded by those trees? But what about you?" The squire frowned and shook his head. "A knight and his lady. Eight horses! You look as if you've been dragged through a thorn hedge backward."

The squire gave Sir Geraint

and Lady Enid as much to eat and drink as they wished, then invited them to the count's castle, where they could wash and rest and feed their horses.

||||||||||||||||||||||||||||||||||||||

The young Count of Limors was used to getting his own way.

None of the knights and squires in service to him, and none of the servants who worked at the castle, liked him in the least, but they remained loyal to him because they were so afraid of him.

King Arthur had heard all about this count: the way he abused and even violated the ladies and unmarried young women in the castle, the way he ignored and insulted his knights and squires.

"Some of my English knights are troublesome enough," Arthur had complained at a meeting of the Round Table, "but seven or eight of my counts and barons in France are even worse."

"You must raise a force and defeat them," Sir Kay had told him.

"And by all accounts," said Sir Bedivere, "Limors is the worst of them all. He's repulsive!"

"The most shameless and brazen are often the most cowardly," Sir Kay had said.

At Limors, the oily young count invited Sir Geraint to tell him about the purpose of his journey. As he listened, he kept smoothing his neatly trimmed beard. Then he asked Geraint's permission to sit with Lady Enid so she might tell him about their journey.

"A wife and husband," he mused with a charming smile, "they rarely view things in exactly the same way."

But the young count didn't ask Enid a single question about their journey. Not one.

"I've never seen a knight treat his wife so shabbily," he said to her in a low, confiding voice, and he laid a manicured finger on her wrist. "Dragging you such a distance. Without proper protection. Without shelter or food and drink. Whom does Sir Geraint think you are?"

Lady Enid lowered her eyes. "It's my fault," she said.

"Nonsense," the count replied briskly. "Nothing is ever a beautiful woman's fault, and I've never seen anyone as beautiful as you." He stroked Enid's slender wrist with his finger. "It's quite plain the man doesn't care about you at all. Think about staying here, Enid." He paused. "Think what it could be like if you were my wife."

Enid sat bolt upright. "Never!" she protested.

The count sighed and peered around to make sure Sir Geraint hadn't heard her.

"I'd never betray my husband," Enid said, her eyes flashing.

"I see," said the count, shaking his head. "Well in that case . . . I'm going to kill him. Here and now."

"No!"

"No?"

"You can't kill a defenseless man," Enid whispered hoarsely.

"Then what will it be, Enid?"

Lady Enid froze; she burned. She saw that she and her husband were in the most desperate danger. And she decided the only way to escape was through pretense.

"You're right," she said slowly, softly. "I'm weary of my husband. I don't love him; I don't even like him very much."

"You were born under a lucky star," the count told her.

"I can see that you're strong," said Enid, laying a hand on the count's shoulder. "But I can also see that you'd treat me tenderly." She hesitated. "I'll tell you what. Send two of your armed men to our room at dawn to capture me. My husband's nothing if not brave; he'll try to defend me. But two men can easily cut him down. They can lop off his head, for all I care."

That long night, Enid lay awake, watching over her husband. Then

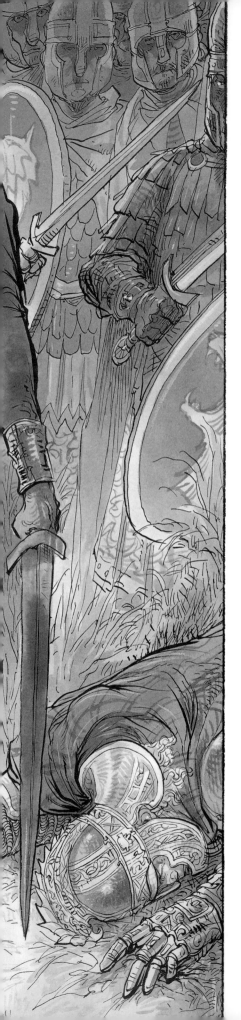

just before dawn, she woke Geraint and told him about the count and his infatuation with her, and how she had tricked him, and how they must escape at once. Hurriedly they dressed. They didn't even risk untying the eight horses they had captured, but simply mounted their own courser and palfrey.

At dawn, the count's armed servants discovered that their guests had escaped and woke their master. At once, the count alerted his grooms, rallied several dozen followers, and set off in pursuit. Through the woods and down the hill. Up the valley. Past the September fields.

At the top of the valley, they caught up with Sir Geraint and Lady Enid. The count's followers struck Geraint's shield with their swords, then they jabbed at his ribs and stabbed his legs until Geraint moaned and fell off his horse sideways.

Pale-faced and motionless, he lay in the long, damp grass.

Lady Enid crouched at the base of a weeping willow and buried her face in her hands.

"Dead!" she sobbed. "He's dead! I'm my own husband's murderer."

"It's right for you to grieve," the young count told her. "It's only natural. But you're going to be a countess now. You're going to be my wife."

"I wish I were dead myself," whispered Enid.

"You're very foolish," said the young count.

He ordered his men to escort Lady Enid back to his castle and to make a simple litter for Sir Geraint's body. They carried the body all the way back and laid it on a bier in the middle of the great hall.

Then the count told his chaplain, "I want to marry Lady Enid at once. I've never desired anyone so much."

The chaplain was just as afraid of his master as everyone else. "I understand," he said. "God will understand."

Before long, a great crowd gathered in the hall. They milled around

Sir Geraint's bloodstained body, his battered shield covering his chest and his sword in its scabbard resting beside him. And there and then, in front of her husband's body, despite her objections and tears and absolute refusal to make any vows, the Count of Limors married Lady Enid.

"We're husband and wife now," he told her. "So don't waste any more of your sweet breath."

Then the count led Enid and all his followers to vespers in the castle chapel. By the time they returned, the steward had arranged for trestles to be set up around Sir Geraint's body, and the tables to be laid for a wedding feast.

Enid refused to eat or drink a morsel.

"Come, now, Enid," the count cajoled, and laid against her lower lip a wild strawberry.

Enid closed her eyes.

"Come!" said the count, and he offered her delicacies——breast of lark, pickled mussels, dates, licorice.

Enid kept her lips shut tightly.

The count finally lost his temper.

"All right!" he shouted, and raised his hand and slapped Enid on the left cheek.

For a moment there was silence. Then one of the count's knights said, "Sire, you can scarcely expect Enid to eat and drink in front of the body of her dead husband."

"I'm her husband!" retorted the count. "Who do you think you are, telling me what I can and can't do?"

The knight's words, however, unlocked feelings shared by everyone in service to the Count of Limors. All around him, people began to grumble and to object to his selfishness and cruelty. Soon the grumbling turned to shouting.

And how did the count respond? first he yelled, "Silence! SILENCE! Enid, she's mine, and I'll do what I like."

Then he raised his hand and smacked her again. Enid cried out, and her left cheek flared like a scarlet rose.

True, the young man lying on the bier may have curled a little toe or even twitched a little finger, but no one noticed.

True, he may have become aware of the babble and wash of voices all around him, but they seemed to come from far away, and he had no sense at all of where he was.

But when the young man heard his wife's cry, it pierced him and woke him. He had to save her.

Cautiously, he half opened one eye and edged his right hand closer to the pommel of his sword.

Then in one swift, single movement, Sir Geraint swung himself down from the bier, and unsheathed his sword. With a terrible shout, he lunged at the count, and with one clean swipe, cut off his head so that brains and blood splattered the feasting tables all around him.

The wedding guests ducked, they dived, they collided with the benches and knocked them over. They ran toward the doors, yelling, "A dead man! A devil! A demon! A dead man!"

Sir Geraint ignored them. He had only one thought. He put his right arm around Enid's shoulders, picked up his battered shield, and hurried her out of the great hall.

By chance, a stable boy had just come into the courtyard with Sir Geraint's own charger to water him. When he saw the knight he was aghast and at once dropped the horse's reins and ran away.

With a painful groan, Sir Geraint hoisted himself into the saddle, then helped Enid up to sit in front of him.

Away they galloped, husband and wife, under the bright moon, which flowered and shone even brighter at the sight of them.

|||||||||||||||||||||||||||||||

The journey back was neither short
nor easy.

Sir Geraint had to fight a giant
whose weapon, like the giant
of Mont-Saint-Michel, was a
monstrous club. Then he and
Enid had to battle blustering
winds from the north and
drenching rainstorms. At last,
they found shelter in an open-
sided barn and burrowed
down into a warm bed of
sweet-smelling hay.

That's where Geraint told
Enid how deeply he loved her and
where Enid told her husband how deeply
she loved him.

"If I didn't love you so," she
whispered, "I wouldn't have spoken a
word."

"And if I hadn't so wanted to prove
myself to you," Geraint replied, "I
wouldn't have ordered you to be silent."

Each had endured so much for the
other: he for her, she for him. There,
in that hay barn, they renewed their

vows and were so joyous together, it was as if neither of them had suffered at all.

Onward they rode, both on the same faithful charger; they rode for seven days. When at last they reached Caerleon, they discovered not only that Geraint's father had just died but also that King Arthur had taken his court to Nantes, in Brittany, a full month before.

So what with the funeral service and the days of mourning that followed, more time passed before Geraint and Enid were able to set off for Nantes.

King Arthur greeted them joyfully, and he rewarded Sir Geraint for proving himself as both a knight and a husband by giving him the most wonderful cloak, generations old and made by four fairies.

On the outside, stitched in gold thread, were four full-length figures portraying Geometry and Arithmetic and Music and Astronomy. The inside of the cloak was lined with the pelts of creatures who live in India. Creatures whose heads are as white as skimmed milk, whose graceful necks are the color of blackberries, whose backs are scarlet, whose stomachs are as green as grass, and whose tails are sky blue.

"All I know about these creatures," the king told Sir Geraint, "is that they survive on expensive spices and cinnamon and fresh cloves and that they're called barbioletes."

King Arthur held a great feast to welcome Sir Geraint and Lady Enid. They sat at the high table with Queen Guinevere, Sir Lancelot, and the king's nephew, Sir Gawain——and with Merlin.

"Love is no tournament," Merlin said solemnly. "It's not a contest you can win or lose. It's a challenge you must face together, with rewards you share."

Enid lowered her eyes and smiled.

Queen Guinevere gave King Arthur a loving smile, then turned to Sir Geraint. "My all-or-nothing knight!" she exclaimed. ||||||||||

VI

|| THE TRIAL OF HONOR ||

Sir Gawain and the Green Knight

It was Christmas Eve at Camelot.

Two years and more had passed since Sir Geraint and Lady Enid had proven their love, seven years since the king had fought with the giant on Mont-Saint-Michel, and almost ten years since young Arthur had pulled the sword from the stone.

The stone walls of the great hall at Camelot were decorated with branches of prickly he-holly and smooth-leaved she-holly with scarlet berries. Pale-eyed sprigs of mistletoe watched over each of the trestle tables. Fir trees and holm oak saplings, taller than the tallest knights, guarded the alcoves and each corner of the hall.

High over the knights and ladies and squires sitting at their places, a superb kissing bough, constructed of curved willow branches and wispy strands of white wool, slowly turned on twisted gold wire.

King Arthur looked over at his harpist, nodded, and raised his right hand. Everyone stood and sang:

"Lady, we thank you
With hearts meek and mild
For the blessing you have given us
With your sweet child."

"We gather here each Christmas Eve," Arthur called out once everyone

was seated again, "to honor the baby born of the virgin, the baby born to redeem us. Friends and families—— especially families!——have their disagreements, or worse. It's true. But on the miracle of our salvation, we can all agree."

A good many knights and ladies nodded or sighed. A few tapped their fingers lightly on the tabletops, thinking of the tensions and disputes under their own roofs. Queen Ygerna's youngest daughter, Morgan, for instance, sitting there at the Christmas Eve feast, was still in love with Arthur, her own half-brother, was still bitterly angry with him, and was still jealous of Guinevere. And why was Morgan's lover, Sir Accolon, always so shifty? And how often had the very greatest of knights, Sir Lancelot, and Guinevere held each other's gaze for a little longer than they should have?

"Each year we gather," the king went on, "not only to honor Jesus but also to honor one another. Here, in this hall,

I've heard of breathtaking adventures during the last twelve months. I've also witnessed the saddest and most shocking sight of my life: my beloved nephew Gawain riding in with the head of an innocent lady, Saraide, hanging around his neck."

The king and his knights and ladies and squires all bowed their heads. Sir Gawain alone sat unbowed.

"You all know how it came about," Arthur said, "this most terrible mistake. On his quest to kill the twenty-pointed White Stag, Sir Gawain rode straight into the hall of Sir Blamoure of the Marsh. Sir Blamoure attacked Gawain, but Gawain forced him to his knees and whirled his sword to behead him. At that very moment, Lady Saraide threw herself in front of her husband to shield him. And so Sir Gawain cut off her head instead." King Arthur paused. "You also know the sentence that Queen Guinevere and a jury of ladies of this court have passed on Sir Gawain."

"Lady Laudine," interjected the

queen, "and the ladies Lyonesse and Lynette."

King Arthur nodded. "Henceforth, Sir Gawain must always take up arms to defend any lady who believes she has been wronged and how, when he fights, he must always be prepared to show mercy.

"We must never take the law into our own hands," King Arthur went on, "but uphold the common good. That's what my chosen knights and I have all pledged. Let us believe the best of one another, as I certainly believe of Sir Gawain. Let us trust and be trustworthy. Let us be chaste and be merciful. Let us be honorable."

"And that is the third trial," Merlin announced. "The third trial of all the knights of the Round Table: the trial of honor, of everything that honor means and requires."

"As you know," the king announced, "it's my habit never to eat or drink at a feast before I've heard or seen a wonder . . . Not that my cooks approve. They complain that I'm spoiling the wild boar, and a hundred delicacies."

"I can tell you a wonder," Queen Guinevere said, "about a triple rainbow."

"No!" Sir Dagonet called out. "I'll tell you all a joke instead. A triple joke!"

"It'll be a wonder if you don't," Merlin growled. "Stop him, someone!"

"I'll tell you about the Yelping Beast," Sir Pellinore offered, "who has the haunches of a lion and the body of a leopard and a hart's delicate feet. Not only that! When he roars, it sounds like thunder."

At the far end of the great hall, the double doors boomed. Then they rattled and sprang open.

Right into the middle of the hall rode a colossal, towering man, as bulky as a troll.

Everyone stared at him, and many of them covered their eyes.

The man was green. Bright green.

His face, his hands, his bushy beard, his surcoat and tunic and

stockings and boots, his belt embroidered with birds and butterflies, were every kind of green: mossy green, luminous willow green, bilious green, jade, emerald, olive, and glistening dark ivy.

So too was this knight's snorting charger: his tackle, the braids on his mane, and the bands and little bells decorating his tail were leek green, gray green, silver green, golden green.

This green man rode right up to the dais, carrying a sprig of he-holly in his left hand and a battle-ax in his right. The blade was more than three feet long, and as sharp as a razor.

"Pff!" he spat. "Look at you all! What a bunch!"

King Arthur stood and faced him.

"Who's your leader?" the Green Knight demanded.

"I am King Arthur," the king replied courteously, "and you're welcome here."

The Green Knight roared with laughter. "Welcome, am I?"

"You're welcome," the king calmly repeated.

"You've no need to be afraid. As you see, I'm not wearing armor. I come in peace," the Green Knight said, twirling his sprig of holly. "I've just stopped by to play a Christmas game with you."

"Eat with us here and now," said the king, "and we'll play your game tomorrow morning."

The Green Knight swatted Arthur's words away. "I've got better things to do than stay around here," he replied. "We'll play this game here and now."

King Arthur chose to ignore the Green Knight's manner. He didn't want to pick a fight.

"This game," said the Green Knight. "I call it 'Off with his head! Alive then dead.'"

He laughed in the faces of all the knights and ladies sitting at the dais. "Whoever plays this game——this beheading game——with me is welcome to use my battle-ax to strike me one blow. Then, in a year and a day, he must come and find me, and bare his neck, and allow me to strike him."

No one spoke. No one looked at

the Green Knight. They all knew that no man could defeat magic, however brave he might be.

The Green Knight rolled his red eyes and burst out laughing. "Not one of you?" he demanded. "You lily-livered lot!" Then he coughed. "Knights of the Round Table! Is that what you are? I'd have thought better of you."

King Arthur gritted his teeth. "All right," he said. "I'll play your game. Give me your battle-ax!"

At once, the Green Knight swung down from his saddle and handed his ax to the king. Arthur swung it a couple of times to judge its weight, while the knight ran his fingers through his beard, coughed again, then bared his green neck.

"No!" shouted Sir Gawain. "Arthur mustn't play this deadly game. He's our king! I'll play it for us all."

"Make up your minds!" the Green Knight snapped. "I haven't got all day."

Sir Gawain took the ax from the king.

"Your name, sire?" inquired the Green Knight.

"Gawain. And after twelve months and a day, where will I find you?"

"All in good time!" the Green Knight told him. "Strike me first."

So Sir Gawain put his left foot a little in front of his right. He gripped the green battle-ax, swung it, and the blade bit cleanly through the Green Knight's neck bone and cut off his head.

The bloody head rolled under the high table, and several knights tried to kick it away.

The Green Knight stepped forward, bent down, and reached for his head. He picked it up and swung back into the saddle of his charger. There he sat, holding his head up high in his right hand. Its eyelids opened and it glared at the silent knights and ladies and squires. Then it cleared its throat.

"Do as you promised, Gawain," the head spluttered. "Come and find me after twelve months on New Year's Day. I'll be at the Green Chapel."

Then the Green Knight wheeled away

from the high table, still holding his head up by its hair. As he rode out through the double doorway into the courtyard, his horse's hooves struck sparks from the flint paving.

| | | | | | | | | | | | | | | | | | | | | | | | | | | | | | | | | | | | | | |

How swiftly the months and seasons of the year passed, especially for Sir Gawain.

Frost again. Frazil ice. The first days of winter. The hedgerows shone with rose hips and clusters of little scarlet berries and copper beech leaves, as if they were already starting to prepare for Christmas themselves.

North wind knifed straight down the spine of Britain, then sliced along the stone corridors of Camelot, even snuffing out some of the candles inside the great hall.

Sir Gawain turned to face the cruel wind and knew that his journey and its ending would likely be worse. Much worse.

Fully armed and riding Gringolet, his stallion that had once belonged to a fairy man, he swept out of Camelot on a tide of tears and pride at his courage and prayers for his safety. He rode north and west toward the Welsh Marches, and whenever he met anyone, he greeted them and inquired whether they knew the way to the Green Chapel. No one had even heard of it.

On he rode into the wilderness of North Wales, where he had no choice but to sleep in the open night after night. He heard the howling of a pack of wolves and thought they had encircled him. At one point, he had to fight three man-eating ogres. The ogres were almost as tall as pine trees, but he hacked away their legs from under them and left them screeching.

When he reached the Wirral, Sir Gawain was surrounded by a group of wild men armed with clubs. Heaven knows how long they'd roamed the forests——outsiders, outcasts——trapping and roasting rabbits and hedgehogs and little birds, eating leaves and berries.

In his warm heart, Sir Gawain felt pity for them, and didn't use his sword against them. He warded off their blows with his shield, spurred Gringolet, and galloped on.

Dear God, he thought, wolves, ogres, wild men . . . all before I even reach the Green Chapel to face the Green Knight.

That night, it rained. At dawn, it grew colder. Around him, the forest world became quiet, somehow very attentive and very still. Not a mouthful of wind. Not a single bird cheeped, even to complain.

And that's when, through the old oak trees ahead of him, Sir Gawain saw a chalk-white castle. Its pinnacles and parapets and towers looked as if they'd been cut out of paper or painted onto the sky.

Sir Gawain reined in, he marveled at its beauty. Then he spurred Gringolet and cantered up to the moat and drawbridge.

At once, a watchman raised the portcullis and waved him welcome, and it wasn't at all long before Sir Gawain had handed Gringolet over to helpful grooms in the stables, was ushered indoors and led straight to a bath of steaming water. There he soaked and daydreamed. With mutton-fat soap, he washed away the sweat and grit and grime of his journey; then two servants handed him shaggy towels, dressed him in brightly colored clothing, and led him into the castle hall.

Almost at once, the lord of the castle strode in——he was thickset and a good head taller than Sir Gawain, with a wind-scorched face, peeling nose, and tangled red beard.

"Welcome!" he boomed, and took Sir Gawain's hands between his own big rough hands. "Welcome! What brings you into our wilderness? And on Christmas Eve at that!"

But before Sir Gawain could say a word, his host exclaimed, "Wait! You haven't yet eaten, have you? Sit here, at this table, and I'll sit beside you. You must forgive us, but we eat so early here in the Wirral. There's really little else to do!"

Servants brought in several fish dishes——salmon and herring and river trout and even little brown shrimp.

"Fasting today!" announced the lord, wiping his nose with the back of his hand. "Feasting tomorrow."

When at last Sir Gawain told the host his name, the lord of the castle rocked back on his bench with delight. "You? You're Sir Gawain? Great Sir Gawain of the Round Table, here with us for our humble Christmas feast. What an honor!"

"I'm indebted to you, sire," Sir Gawain said, bowing his head. "I'll be glad to stay with you tonight, and tomorrow too, but on the day after Christmas, I must ride on."

"Ride on?" the lord of the castle repeated. "Why? Where are you going?"

"The Green Chapel," replied Sir Gawain, "and I don't even know where it is. But on New Year's Day, I have a meeting there."

At this moment, two ladies came into the hall. Sir Gawain caught his breath. One of the ladies, the host's wife, was as lovely a woman as ever you're likely to see, her movements so graceful, her lips half smiling, her eyes green.

She's even more lovely than Guinevere, Gawain thought.

The other lady was a great deal older, her cheeks wrinkled and gray. Her thick black eyebrows were untrimmed, her chin was rather hairy, and she smelled sour.

The lord of the castle led Sir Gawain over to meet them. The knight first bowed courteously to the older woman and then kissed his host's wife on each cheek.

"You're just in time, ladies," the lord of the castle said. "Sir Gawain was just telling me that he doesn't know where the Green Chapel is."

"Doesn't know?" warbled the older woman. "It's only a mile away."

"If it's more than one, it's certainly less than two," the host agreed. "Sir Gawain, you're most welcome to stay here until New Year's morning. After your long journey, you need rest."

Sir Gawain took a deep breath. All at once, he felt so tired.

"I always go out hunting on the last three days of the year," the lord of the castle continued, "but you must lie low. Eat, sleep, drink, do whatever you like. If you want company, my wife will gladly entertain you." He rubbed his rough hands. "I'll tell you what. We can play a little game. Let's exchange gifts. Whatever I bring back from the forest, I'll give to you. And if you win anything here, you can give it to me."

"By all means," said Sir Gawain with a smile, and then yawned.

"Excellent!" said his host, and he emptied his beaker of wine. "Lead our guest to his room," he instructed his servants. "Poor man! He can scarcely stay awake."

Two men with flaming torches showed Sir Gawain the way along shadowy corridors into the heart of the castle.

The splendid guest room was so peaceful, so still, that after Gawain had put on his nightshirt and climbed into the four-poster bed, he could hear his own heart beating.

| | | | | | | | | | | | | | | | | | | | | | | | | | | | | | | | | | | | | | | | | | | | | |

Sir Gawain slept well and deeply. Nevertheless, when his bedroom door creaked open just after dawn, he awoke at once.

Pretending he was still asleep, Gawain peered between his fingers and the narrow opening between the damask curtains of his four-poster bed, and saw that his host's wife had slipped into the room. He watched as she stole toward him, parted the curtains, and sat down lightly on the edge of his bed.

Gawain closed his eyes again and lay motionless, still feigning sleep. There she sat for a very long while, looking at him, waiting for him to wake . . .

At last, the knight opened his eyes, made a great show of stretching, and turned to face the lady.

"How careless you are," she said with an enchanting smile, "allowing me to slip into your room. You're my captive now. I'm going to keep you imprisoned in this room."

"My lady," Sir Gawain replied, "allow me to rise and get dressed. Then we can keep each other company all morning."

"No, no. I'm going to keep you here in this bed," the lady said. "After all, we're all alone and won't be disturbed."

So that's what happened. They talked all morning——Sir Gawain still tucked up in bed and the host's wife sitting on the edge of it.

At long last, she stood and said, "Well, you have certainly been courteous and mannerly. But . . . aren't you even going to ask me for a kiss?"

"Certainly," Sir Gawain replied.

So the lady leaned down, took Sir Gawain in her arms, and gave him a loving kiss.

That evening, Sir Gawain wrapped his arms around his host's neck, and kissed him on the cheek.

The lord of the castle raised his bushy eyebrows. "A kiss! Really! Where did that come from?"

Sir Gawain smiled. "We agreed to exchange our winnings, not to say

where they came from," he said. "That wasn't part of our bargain."

"You have me there!" his host brayed. Then he cleared his throat and slapped Sir Gawain on the back. "Still, that won't stop me from telling you how I won your gift."

The very next moment, two servants came in bearing venison on silver trays, one portion already roasted, the other raw.

"This meat is from the loveliest does I've seen in years," said the host, and he patted the raw meat with both hands. "Plump in the right parts, lean in the right parts."

Joyously, he launched into a description not only of pursuing the deer, and of how his hounds had torn them apart, but also of how his men had undressed them——their offals and stomachs and bowels and gullets and windpipes and weasends and numbles and chines.

"All for you, Gawain," he announced. "It's all yours!"

Never once taking her dancing eyes

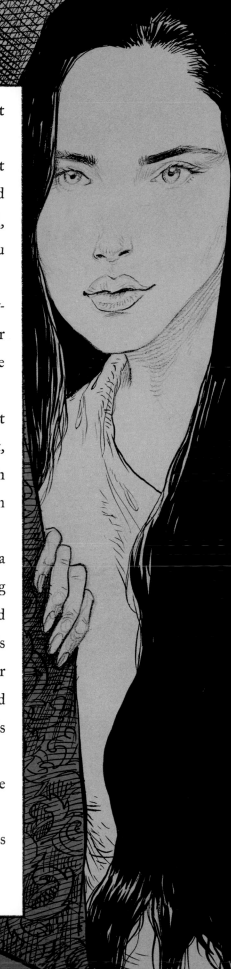

off Sir Gawain, the host's wife stole up behind her husband and wrapped her arms around him.

"You're so skillful and strong," she said to him, laughing. "Nothing can withstand you."

"True enough!" the host exclaimed. "Now let's eat. We're all famished." The host gestured to a servant to sound his hunting horn. Immediately, a legion of kitchen boys began carrying in all kinds of spices and sauces to accompany the venison, along with stuffing, carrots, sliced onions, and flagons of red wine. All feasted till they were satisfied.

Early on the second morning, Sir Gawain was already awake when the host's wife crept into his room.

At once she sat beside him on the bed and sweetly reproved him. "Where are your manners? You seem to have forgotten what I taught you yesterday."

"What, my lady?"

"Don't you remember? By way of greeting, you should ask me for a kiss."

"I didn't dare to, my lady," Sir Gawain replied, "for fear you would refuse me."

"Who could refuse you anything?" the lady said, and she kissed the knight on the cheek.

All morning, Sir Gawain and the host's wife talked, mostly about the rules of love. When she stood to take her leave, she gave Sir Gawain a loving kiss as she'd done on the previous day.

On the second day that he went hunting, the lord of the castle and his followers were able to corner a wild boar, and although it impaled three hounds on its sharp tusks, it couldn't withstand the hail of arrows.

"He was foaming!" blared the host along the dinner table. "Foaming! But we peppered him. He grunted, he snorted, he pricked up his ears. My hounds yelped. My men blew their horns. And he's my second gift to you."

Servants then carried in the head of the magnificent boar, with an apple in its mouth and wearing a garland of bay and rosemary. Everyone in the hall sang:

"Hey! Hey! Hey! Hey!
Off with his head!
Armed with rosemary and with bay.
Grunting, gruesome. Alive then dead!"

"Yes," said the host. "He's my second gift to you, Gawain. But what about you? Did you win anything here today?"

At once Sir Gawain put his arms around his host's neck and kissed him on the left cheek, then on his right. He knew very well that the lord's wife was looking straight at him, maybe smiling, but he lowered his eyes to avoid returning her gaze.

"Really?" exclaimed his host. "Two kisses!"

"Two kisses," repeated Sir Gawain.

"If you go on like this," said the lord of the castle, "you'll grow rich. Where did you get them from?"

But Sir Gawain just shook his head, smiled, and said nothing.

On New Year's Eve——the third and last day that the lord went hunting——his beautiful wife hurried along the shadowy corridors into the heart of the castle and stole into Sir Gawain's hushed bedroom for a third time. Then she peeked through the curtain of his four-poster bed.

"Good morning, Sir Gawain!" she said.

"Good morning, my lady."

"Your lady . . . Your lady. Ah, how I wish I were!"

"You're married to a finer man than I will ever be," Sir Gawain replied. "Had I not sworn to serve my own uncle, King Arthur, I'd gladly serve him."

"I'll serve you instead," the lady said, leaning into him and kissing him on his lips.

"My lady!" exclaimed Sir Gawain rather nervously.

"Ah!" she sighed. "Now I understand: you must have given your heart to another woman. Is that it?"

"No, no!" he protested.

"Well, in that case . . ." she said in a husky voice, snuggling a little closer.

Sir Gawain scarcely knew what to do. His mind was arguing with his heart and body.

"My dear," the host's wife whispered into Sir Gawain's ear, "at least give me a little gift to remember you by."

Sir Gawain frowned. "When I left Camelot," he said, "I didn't pack a saddle bag with gifts for ladies——not a fillet for your hair, nor a breast pin or a mirror."

"Kiss me!" she whispered.

"I cannot," Sir Gawain said. "I must not."

"All right," she whispered, "I'll kiss you then." And that's what she did.

Then the host's wife sighed again. "Will you give me one of your gloves?"

"A glove!" repeated Sir Gawain, feeling rather breathless. "A well-thumbed glove? That's scarcely a gift for a beautiful woman."

"Well, then, I'll give you another gift. I'll give you a ring."

The knight shook his head. "No, my lady."

"I say yes," the lady whispered, and she laid her fingertips on his chest. "I know! I've a better idea."

Then she untied the long girdle from

around her slender waist and held it up. It was made of green silk, green as new grass, embroidered with gold.

"I'm not worthy of it," Sir Gawain told her. "Not until I've ridden to the Green Chapel and fulfilled my promise."

"Oh!" cried the lady. "Because it's such a simple little thing? Just a rag, really."

"No, no!" said Sir Gawain. "It's not that."

The lady sat up. "I know it's not much to look at," she said in a low voice, "but whoever wears this girdle can never be badly hurt. No weapon can wound him; no kind of magic can injure him."

The moment Sir Gawain heard the lady's words, he recalled his meeting with the Green Knight. He hesitated, and under his bedclothes he trembled just a little.

"My lady," he said very slowly, "I will accept it. I'll wind it around my waist and wear it as a token of your love."

The host's wife stroked his right cheek. "Just promise," she said.

"Promise me you won't tell anyone I've given it to you."

Then she kissed Sir Gawain for a third time. With her green eyes, she gazed at him. For how long? For a few seconds? Forever. Then she stood and slipped out of the room.

That evening, the lord of the castle and his guest met in the hall by the blazing hearth, and Sir Gawain lost no time at all in embracing his host and kissing him three times.

"Three kisses!" exclaimed the lord, tugging at his matted red beard.

"Three kisses," Sir Gawain repeated.

"You've done better than I have." He beckoned to a servant, and the man stepped forward with the tawny pelt of a fox and gave it to the knight.

"Yes, a mangy fox," said the host. "Very clever. Very sly. But I outwitted him in the end."

Sir Gawain thanked him. "Three beautiful does, a wild boar, a wily fox," he said. "One kiss, two kisses, three kisses."

"And that's all?" his host asked.

"Three kisses," Sir Gawain repeated.

"Well," said his host, "you're the winner. What can possibly compare with loving kisses?"

The fire in the hearth flickered orange and green.

"As you know," Sir Gawain told his host, "I must ride to the Green Chapel early in the morning."

"I've asked one of my men to show you the way."

Then Sir Gawain went from servant to servant, making a point of remembering each of their names and thanking them for their service, before turning to the lord's wife and her withered old companion, and lastly to the lord of the castle himself, embracing each of them.

With his head and heart brimming but his words hesitant, he thanked his host for honoring him with such a wonderfully warm welcome and such hospitality.

"These days," he said. "Long or short as my life may be, I will never forget them."

Then, as before, two servants with

flaming torches led Sir Gawain for a last time to his room. But when he climbed into the chilly bed, he lay wide awake, crushed between his sense of dishonor at accepting the gift of the lady's girdle and his trepidation at meeting the Green Knight. When at last he did fall asleep, he had terrifying nightmares and woke several times in a cold sweat.

|||||||||||||||||||||||||||||||||||||||||

"See that cliff?" said the watchman. "Keep it on your right. Ride down through these trees to the bottom of the valley, and you'll see a waterfall and a pool that looks as if it's boiling. Near it is a big green mound, an old burial place."

Sir Gawain wiped the rain from his eyes and rubbed Gringolet's neck.

"Except . . ." said the watchman.

"What?"

"I wouldn't go near the place myself. Not even if I had nine lives. There's a Green Knight down there . . ."

"I know," said Sir Gawain.

"I wouldn't tell my master or anyone . . ."

"If I sneak off, you mean. Who do you think I am?" the knight protested.

"Suit yourself, then," the watchman said abruptly, and with that, he wheeled his hackney and headed back toward the castle.

At the bottom of the valley, Sir Gawain dismounted and tied Gringolet to the branch of a sopping linden tree. Slowly, he approached the green mound and walked all around it. He put his head inside the three dark openings——one at one end and one on each side of it—— but they were stopped up with earth and led nowhere. Then he scrambled to the top of the mound.

Can this be it? He wondered. Can this really be the Green Chapel? It's deserted.

What with his coat of mail and gauntlets and shin guards and thigh pieces and arm pieces——and with the green silk belt securely wound twice around his waist——Sir Gawain was wonderfully well armed, but he could

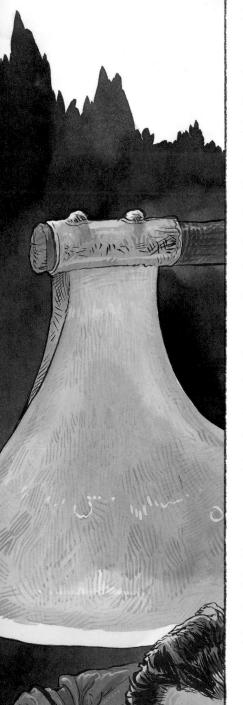

still feel the rain seeping down the back of his neck and working its way into his steel sabatons and between his toes.

He stood motionless, he waited, and he shivered.

Then, from somewhere up on the cliff in the shining mist, dozens of stones and rocks came barreling and leaping toward him down the steep slope. After this there was a terrible clatter, and with a mighty shout, the Green Knight himself came bounding down the slope. He leaped across the waterfall and, swinging his ax, strode up to Sir Gawain.

"Welcome!" he boomed, and just for a moment sounded almost friendly. But then he glared at Sir Gawain. "You're a man of your word," he barked, "and I won't keep you waiting. 'Off with your head! Alive then dead!'"

"I'm ready," Sir Gawain replied.

The Green Knight ran his left forefinger along the sharp blade of his huge ax. "Take off your helmet, then, and bare your neck . . . Yes . . . now bow your head."

As the Green Knight raised his ax, Sir Gawain glanced sideways and a little upward, and the Green Knight at once stayed his hand. "Afraid, are you?" he growled.

"I won't flinch again."

The Green Knight raised his ax again, and this time Sir Gawain kept stock-still. But, when the blade was just an inch from Sir Gawain's neck, the Green Knight stayed his hand for a second time. "Ah! That's better," he exclaimed. "I can see you're ready now."

The Green Knight raised his huge ax for a third time, then he brought it winging down.

The Green Knight struck Sir Gawain in such a way that the blade only just grazed his neck. Spots of bright blood spattered the ground in front of him.

At once he leaped sideways, snatched up his helmet, and drew his sword.

The Green Knight laughed and held up his left hand. "Easy does it!" he said.

"I've kept my word," Sir Gawain gasped. "And you've struck me."

"It's true. You've kept your word.

Now listen to me! My first two feints . . . Well, twice I stayed my hand because twice you gave me all your winnings. One kiss on the first evening, two kisses on the second evening."

Sir Gawain squinted at the Green Knight. In the drizzle and the mist and the gloom, he glowed brighter green than ever: his skin, his beard, his armor, his ax . . .

"On the third evening," the Green Knight went on, "you gave me three kisses but didn't fully honor our bargain. You didn't give me that green girdle, did you?"

Sir Gawain lowered his eyes. He lowered his head.

"I know that girdle," the Green Knight told him. "It belongs to my wife. Three times I sent her to your bedroom to test you."

"And I failed! I failed!" Sir Gawain lamented. He grabbed the girdle and hurled it at the Green Knight's feet, then lowered his head again.

"No," the Green Knight slowly replied. "No, Sir Gawain, you didn't fail."

And when Sir Gawain raised his eyes once more, standing in front of him was not the terrifying Green Knight but the jovial, bushy-bearded lord of the castle, with his rosy face and peeling nose.

"Why did you accept the girdle from my wife?" the Green Knight went on. "Not because you were greedy, not because you were lustful, and not because you were dishonorable, but simply because you love your life. You say you failed; I say you did not fail but, because you didn't give me the girdle, you didn't wholly succeed."

The lord of the castle picked up the girdle. "Take it," he said. "Wear it, and it will remind you of our meeting."

"It will remind me of my failure," Sir Gawain replied. "My unworthiness."

"And now," the lord invited, "come straight back to my castle. Let's eat and drink and laugh together. Let us bring in this New Year with music."

Sir Gawain shook his head. "Sire," he said, "I've been away for so long. I must ride back to Camelot. But before I go, please tell me your name."

"Sir Bertilak of the High Peak. Some old people say Sir Bertilak de Hautdesert."

"And that old woman who keeps you and your wife company? Who is she?"

Sir Bertilak nodded and smiled. "Her name is Morgan le Fay."

"Morgan! Not the king's half sister?"

"Yes, she lives with us. She uses her magic to disguise herself by looking ancient."

Sir Gawain shook his head and frowned.

"It was she who asked me to ride to Camelot to test the king," Sir Bertilak explained, "and to torment Guinevere. You know how bitter she is about Arthur——how much she hates him."

"How is that possible? She was at Camelot herself when you rode into the great hall."

"Gawain," said Sir Bertilak, "Morgan lives here; she lives on an island called Avalon; she lives with her husband, Sir Urien; she consorts with her admirer Sir Accolon, sometimes she

|| 131 ||

visits Camelot . . . She can be here and not here, just as she wishes."

Then Sir Gawain and Sir Bertilak looked each other in the eye and smiled, both of them reluctant to turn away.

|||||||||||||||||||||||||||||||||

Sir Gawain sang bits of battle songs and love songs; his neck wound began to heal; aconites and snowdrops sprang up around Gringolet's hooves.

Because so few people at Camelot had dared hope that he would ever return from his terrifying assignment at the Green Chapel, the court's joy was all the greater.

And no one's joy exceeded that of his uncle, King Arthur.

In the great hall, Sir Gawain recounted his journey and bargain with Sir Bertilak, and freely confessed to how he had played him false.

"Because of it," he said, holding the green silk up so that everyone could see it, "I mean to wear this girdle as a reminder of my failure until the day I die."

"Failure?" King Arthur called out. "No! You didn't fail. You've honored us all."

Then the king turned to the knights of the Round Table, opened his arms, and declared, "We'll all wear your girdle," and the knights, they all waved and shouted, and acclaimed Sir Gawain.

"Let each knight wear a grass-green girdle," King Arthur proclaimed, "embroidered with gold, as a sign he's been admitted to our fair fellowship, the fellowship of the knights of the Round Table. And let each of us remember his vow: to be as honorable as any man can be. To be almost perfect, but not quite!"

|||||||||||||||||||||||||||||||||||||

VII

|| THE TRIAL OF MAGIC ||

King Arthur and Sir Accolon

When Sir Gawain told King Arthur that it was his own sister Morgan who sent the Green Knight to Camelot, the king realized quite plainly what danger he was in. Such were Morgan's jealousy and bitterness that he knew how vigilant he had to be.

One May evening, Arthur and Merlin were strolling along the path around the lake at Camelot. After a while, the young king took Merlin's arm. They paused and watched the setting sun stain the water crimson. The magician waved away a ball of gnats spinning and swarming around their heads.

"I think it's true, Merlin, that you're able to fly from one place to another, and even to be in two places at the same time. But is it true that you can fly into people's minds as well?"

"To give them thoughts, you mean?" the magician asked. "Or steal their thoughts?"

"I don't know," said Arthur. "To warn them. To give them hope."

"Not if they don't want me to," Merlin replied. "Only if their minds are open. Why do you ask?"

Arthur withdrew his arm. "There have been times," he said, "like pulling the sword from the stone, and the Lady of the Lake and Excalibur, when I thought you were in my mind."

"You haven't forgotten what I told you," Merlin cautioned him.

"To wear it or keep it beside me day and night," Arthur said. "And to remember the scabbard is more powerful than the sword. No, I haven't forgotten. What I was going to say is that there have been times when I've felt empowered by you. Times when things would have turned out differently, or not worked out at all. But . . ."

"And that's not enough?" the magician inquired. "As I've told you, I'll fly into your mind, if I'm able to."

"What do you mean?"

"What I say."

As they crossed a little footbridge over the moat and climbed a flight of stone steps, Arthur thought how much he still depended on the magician, and how Merlin was spending less and less time with him, and more and more with his bewitching apprentice, Nimue.

He's a magician, thought Arthur, and yet she has him under her spell!

"You and the knights of your Round Table have endured and succeeded in three great trials," Merlin told him. "The trial of friendship and bravery, the trial of love, the trial of honor. But the fourth will be the most grievous: the trial of magic. White magic. Black magic."

||||||||||||||||||||||||||||||||||||||

At the top of the stone steps, two servants were waiting for King Arthur.

"Sire, you have visitors," said the first servant.

"Your own sister," the second man told him. "And her husband."

"Morgan and Sir Urien?" said the king, surprised.

"And Sir Accolon with them," the second servant said.

Arthur raised his eyebrows and smiled. "Her admirer," he said quietly to Merlin. "Wherever she goes, he goes."

"And wherever they go," the magician added, "there's trouble. It would be much better for you and better for Guinevere if your sister never set foot in Camelot again. Her spells and charms can be deadly."

That evening, the king's jester, Sir Dagonet, entertained his guests. Some of the verses he sang sounded rather splendiferous and almost witty:

"A pride of lions.
An unkindness
of ravens,
A skulk of foxes.
An impatience
of wives . . ."

Sir Dagonet sang not only with his voice box but also with his long, mournful face and his waving arms. Whenever he paused, he started to drum his long white fingers on a tabletop.

The jester's jokes were not as good as his songs, and his conjuring tricks were far worse than both. Whatever Morgan and Merlin saw in him was not at all clear, but they all delighted in his tomfoolery and fumbling sleights of hand.

Not that Merlin paid Sir Dagonet his undivided attention. He kept turning to Nimue, who was sitting beside him, and taking her right hand or putting an arm around her shoulders and whispering to her.

Arthur watched the magician. He's not nearly as calm or quiet as he usually is, he thought. He's fretful. He's besotted with her. He can't take his eyes off her or keep his hands off her . . . He's so old; she's so young . . .

The king saw plainly enough that Nimue was asking Merlin one question after another, and from time to time he could hear the old enchanter saying, "I will show you," and, "I will tell you. I will! Be patient."

What the king didn't see, partly perhaps because he didn't want to, was just how many lingering looks his wife, Guinevere, was lavishing on Sir Lancelot, or how attentive and devoted Lancelot was to Guinevere. Had it ever crossed his mind that they might be falling in love? Even if it had, he would have quickly dismissed any possibility that his wife and his greatest knight would betray him.

"You do right to expect the best of everyone," Merlin told Arthur once. "Doing so brings out the best in them. They try to rise to your expectations. Remember, however, that each of us is also a sinner. Each of us is capable of doing great harm, wounding the very people we love most."

On another occasion, the enchanter told Arthur: "The first thing is to observe. What do your eyes tell you? Look, and see. And then listen. Use all your senses like a cat or a dog; use your instinct. And after that, always ask yourself why."

When everyone had at last had enough of Sir Dagonet's nonsense, and his taking dead rabbits out of hats and rats out of ladies' dresses, King Arthur and his guests and courtiers stood up. With kisses and hand clasps, they wished one another a peaceful night, undisturbed by devils or night hags.

"Early tomorrow," the king told his sister Morgan, "your husband and Sir Accolon and I will go hunting."

||||||||||||||||||||||||||||||||||||||||

That night, Morgan sat for some time in an ancient rocking chair, staring fiercely at the blue tip of a flaming candle.

She could hear her husband, Sir Urien, breathing deeply, and when she was sure he was asleep, she tapped her forehead three times, then seven, then nine. Then she murmured something and spread her arms as widely as she could.

Morgan stood up. She padded across the bedroom to the door. She grasped the latch and opened the door. But neither the rocking chair nor the stone floor nor the door nor the latch made the least noise. With magic, she had taken all their sounds away.

Morgan swept back her red hair. Carrying her candle, she glided down a passage and entered the room of her lover, Sir Accolon. For a few moments, she watched, she waited, and then she bent down and picked up his sword.

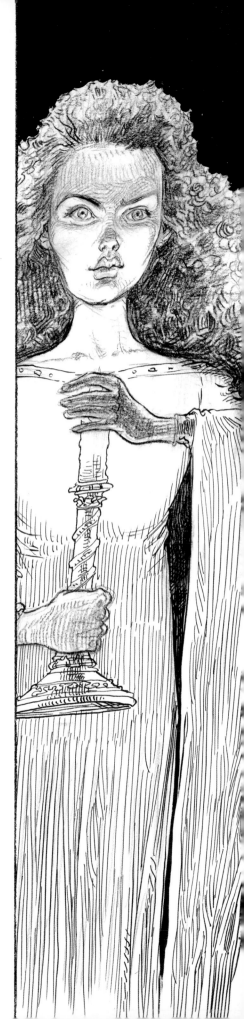

Not a sound. Nothing. Nothing but the ebb and flow of the small night wind; a tawny owl hooting; the sudden, shocking shriek of a rabbit. Sounds beyond even Morgan's reach.

Now the enchantress hurried straight to Arthur and Guinevere's room. Within the tent of their four-poster bed, they were sound asleep too. Morgan smiled. As sound itself sleeps, she thought. As each single sound in Camelot sleeps.

Then she picked up Excalibur and its scabbard, lying just outside the silk drapery enclosing the four-poster bed, quickly replaced it with Sir Accolon's sword, and floated out of the silent room.

Morgan retraced her steps to her sleeping lover's room. She set down Excalibur beside him.

And then, beside her sleeping husband, Sir Urien, she released everything from its prison of silence and blew out her candle.

||||||||||||||||||||||||||||||||

Sir Accolon was scarcely awake when, just after dawn, he felt a warm hand on his right shoulder.

"My love!" he groaned, assuming Morgan was beside him. "My enchantress!"

"Listen to me," a voice whispered in return. "You are going hunting this morning. While you're out, a man is going to come after you, meaning to harm you."

Sir Accolon yawned and sat up.

"He won't know or recognize you, and you won't know or recognize him. You must fight him, Accolon. Show him no mercy."

"No mercy?"

"Wound him and kill him."

"Kill him?" the knight exclaimed.

"If you kill this man, I swear to you that I'll leave Sir Urien and marry you."

Sir Accolon blinked in the darkness and reached out for his lover, but his hands grasped air.

"I'll leave Sir Urien and marry you," the voice said again.

"But . . ."

It was no use. The voice and its owner had gone.

That morning, King Arthur, Sir Urien, Sir Accolon, and their squires cornered and killed a graceful roe deer, but during the afternoon, they were separated from one another, as so often happens. Each could hear yelping horns and yapping hounds well enough, but they seemed to be coming from all around them.

Sir Urien was first to tire of the chase, but not very long after, King Arthur also returned to Camelot.

At once, his sister Morgan ran down a flight of steps and met him as he dismounted.

"Arthur! Arthur!" she cried. "My first love! My always love!"

"Morgan!"

"I've been threatened!" she cried. "And you've been insulted! He said you were weak. A reckling! A runt! He said he spoke for half the knights in the kingdom."

"Who did?" Arthur demanded.

"I know you don't love me——not as I've always loved you——but I'll never hear anyone speak against you."

"Who?" repeated Arthur. "Who said I was weak?"

"How should I know? A knight. He rode right into the great hall. He said you were unworthy."

King Arthur growled.

"And he threatened to use my body." Morgan waved in the direction of the forest. "Send out your men at once. Catch him."

"I'll fight him myself," Arthur told her. "I'm not standing for insults like that. I'll take Merlin with me."

But although the king repeatedly called for the enchanter and sent his servants scurrying around looking for him, there was no sign of him, and no one had seen him all day.

"Merlin!" he called out one last time, and then, more in desperation than hope, "Mer . . . lin!"

He's probably out somewhere with Nimue, thought Arthur. He can't stay away from her.

Then he remounted his destrier,

turned it around, and charged straight back into the forest by himself.

| | | | | | | | | | | | | | | | | | | | | | | | | | | | | | | | | | | | | | | |

The moment King Arthur struck Sir Accolon's shield for the first time, he knew the sword in his hand was not Excalibur.

Then Sir Accolon whacked the king's helmet and rattled his brainpan, so that Arthur couldn't think straight, let alone work out what had happened to his own sword. And when Sir Accolon struck him for a second time, the young king couldn't see straight either. All around him, the gray trunks of the beech trees began to sway.

All the same, King Arthur was able to carve away both Sir Accolon's thigh guards, and then he skinned the knight's right hip. For almost an hour, the two men exchanged blows until, quite suddenly, the blade held by the king snapped, and he was left grasping nothing but the pommel.

"Submit!" growled Sir Accolon. "Down on your knees!"

King Arthur took a step back and held up the pommel. "I can't fight," he said. "Not without a weapon."

"On your knees!"

King Arthur shook his head.

"I'll kill you, then," said Sir Accolon.

"You can't. You can't kill a man who has no weapon."

Then King Arthur saw that Merlin and his apprentice, Nimue, were standing right behind his opponent.

Arthur squeezed his eyes shut. Then he opened them wide. The magician and his apprentice were still there.

Where had they come from?

Arthur had no idea. It was as if they had grown out of the ground or had been there, invisible, the whole time. But the king could see well enough that they stood between his life and his death.

Slowly Nimue raised her right hand level with her shoulder. She pointed her forefinger and fourth finger at Sir Accolon. Then she placed her left hand over her heart. She filled her lungs, and she shrieked.

At once, Excalibur fell from Sir Accolon's hand. When he reached down to retrieve it, he tripped and cried out at the terrible pain in his right hip. King Arthur pounced. He grasped his own sword and felt all its power surging through his body again.

Then the king raised Excalibur in salutation toward Merlin and his apprentice, but they were no longer there. There was no sign of either of them.

"The trial of magic . . . the trial of magic . . ."

The old magician's words rang in Arthur's ears.

Then the king shouted, whirled around, and cut right through Sir Accolon's mail shirt. Excalibur's blade played terrible war music against the knight's ribs.

Again Arthur brandished his blade, and this time he drove its point into the knight's stomach.

Accolon fell over backward, gasping. The king looked down at him.

"Who are you?" he demanded.

"Sir Accolon."

"No!" exclaimed the king, and at once, he fell to his knees.

"Whoever you are," Sir Accolon whispered, "you must go to Camelot. King Arthur will welcome you."

"Whoever I am . . ."

"Yes, he promised me a place at the Round Table. He will grant it to you in my place."

"Whoever I am," the king repeated. Then he pulled off his helmet.

When he saw Arthur's face, Sir Accolon wept. He choked and he wept.

"It's wrong, it's always wrong, not to show mercy," King Arthur said to him, "and worse than that, it's treason to try to kill your king. But you didn't know with whom you were fighting, so I'll spare your life."

"Morgan must have exchanged our swords," Sir Accolon croaked. "I love her, Arthur, I love her so, but you know how she hates you. She says she wants you buried under ten feet of clay."

"Does she, now?" growled Arthur between gritted teeth.

"But I never imagined that she'd set us against each other."

The king bowed his head. He closed his eyes, desolate that his own half sister could hate him so much.

Then Sir Accolon began to choke and gurgle. The king loosened the knight's right gauntlet. Firmly and warmly, he held Accolon's hand until he died.

Later that same day, King Arthur had Sir Accolon's body laid out on a long shield. He sent it to his sister Morgan, who had already left Camelot and was on her way back north to her home with Sir Bertilak and his wife in Hautdesert. The king's messengers told her that the body was a gift from her brother and that he had won back his sword Excalibur and its scabbard.

Very slowly, King Arthur rode to an abbey near Camelot. He showed the nuns there how badly he had been wounded and asked them to bleed him with leeches and look after him while he recovered.

Morgan, meanwhile, shook with sorrow when she saw Sir Accolon's body. She seethed with fury at the king's message. With her husband, Sir Urien, and their train of followers, she turned around and in the morning headed south again. She rode straight to the abbey.

How beautiful it was when she arrived: the warm, yellow evening sun on the limestone walls, throaty doves calling to one another, the white horse chestnut candles shining, and a single bell, slightly flat and tinny like a failing heart, tolling and summoning the nuns to vespers.

The old abbess wasn't altogether sure, but she thought she had heard stories about Morgan and her command of magic, and she was mistrustful.

But what was she to do? Morgan was the king's own half sister, the youngest daughter of Queen Ygerna.

"My dear," the old abbess told Morgan when she reached the abbey, "you cannot talk to him."

Morgan trembled. "He's not dead?"

"Oh, no!" said the abbess. "Praise be to God! No, he's in a deep sleep. He's been asleep since last night. He didn't

even wake up when the bell rang for terce."

"You frightened me," said Morgan. "My poor brother! I'll sit beside him."

"You've been traveling all day, dear. Get some sleep yourself. He'll still be here in the morning."

Morgan stiffened and raked her fingers through her red, red hair. "No," she insisted. "I must see him now."

So the abbess led Morgan through the dappled cloisters to a little cell where in the half-light Arthur lay sleeping. He was holding Excalibur, unsheathed, in his right hand.

Morgan gazed down at him. Then she perched on a stool beside him.

"I'll come back into the cloisters very soon," Morgan whispered to the abbess. "I'll find you there?"

But Morgan did not return to the cloisters. For a long time, she sat watching Arthur, watching and remembering . . . his sweet breath, his warm breathing, the breathing and breaking of the passionate sea around Tintagel, her own heart breaking when

she learned he was to be betrothed to Guinevere, and Guinevere's contempt for her . . .

In the little cell, it grew chill. The failing light coming through the barred window softened the sharp edges of the bed's oak headboard, the chest beside it, the table in the corner, until they were nondescript gray shapes.

A splash of early pinkish-yellow roses in a pottery jar: they alone kept hold of their color in the gloom.

Morgan reached out a hand, intending to ease Excalibur from her brother's grip, but then decided not to, for fear it might wake him. She reached out for a second time and actually managed to touch the blade. But then she picked up the scabbard lying at her feet. She picked it up and fled.

Unable to spirit herself away from the Abbey because it had been blessed and sprinkled with holy water, Morgan could only run. She hurried through the knot garden and past the orderly vegetable beds and over the wild meadow, and only when she reached the blue and charcoal

shadows around the watching trees did she stop and regain her breath.

Morgan carried the scabbard of Excalibur to the same lake where King Arthur had rowed out with Merlin——the lake where he had taken the sword and the scabbard from the white hand holding it up above the water.

In the dark, she caressed the emeralds and rubies inlaid into the gold. Then she grasped the scabbard and hurled it far out into the silent, dark water.

||||||||||||||||||||||||||||

King Arthur had been so badly wounded by Sir Accolon that three weeks passed before he was strong enough to ride back to Camelot from the abbey.

Not long after he had done so, early one June evening, a young woman riding bareback arrived at court. She asked the stable master for an audience with the king and said that she was a messenger from the king's own sister Morgan.

"Arthur grants audiences to anyone and everyone," the stable master told her. "Even a messenger from Morgan. His court is always open to friend and enemy alike."

So the next morning, the young woman entered the great hall. And when it was her turn, she walked up to the king, who was sitting on the throne.

"Your sister Morgan greets you and your queen," she began. "She feels bitter regret, and more than regret, terrible remorse; for causing you such anguish, first by sending Sir Accolon to fight you and then by stealing the scabbard of Excalibur. She has asked me to tell you that she has been out of her mind because of her anguish at the death of Sir Accolon and asks you in all sincerity to forgive her for stealing the scabbard. With her magic, she will raise it from the lake where it now lies and return it to you."

The young woman paused. She has such strange eyes, thought Guinevere. Watchful, troubled eyes . . . I don't know. I don't trust her. Not for one moment.

"In the meantime," the young woman went on, "your sister has sent you a gift."

"A gift," repeated Arthur, recalling that the last gift he had sent to Morgan was Accolon's dead body.

"Or rather," the young woman corrected herself, "a gift for your queen, Lady Guinevere. It's by no means as marvelous as that magical gown you gave to your knight Sir Geraint, but in its own way, it is very wonderful."

Then the young woman unrolled the bundle between her hands and shook it out. It was a cloak with a hood.

The king and queen and Sir Lancelot, who was standing next to them, all inspected it. And then Merlin and Nimue stepped forward and examined it too. It shone and changed color from yellow to bronze to orange, depending on how the light fell on it, but none of them could say what material it was made of.

"Sir Urien didn't know either," the young woman told them. "Morgan told me it wasn't made of wool or linen or silk, but from skin."

"Skin?" Guinevere repeated.

"Crocodile skin."

"What's crocodile?"

"They live in a river in Africa and have horrible teeth and claws," the young woman said. "But their dung is beautifully scented, and their skin is mainly the color of yellow crocus."

"Well," said King Arthur. "No cloak on earth could make my queen more beautiful than she already is. But all the same . . . try it on, Guinevere."

"Willingly," said Guinevere.

"No!" Merlin said sharply. "No! Let the girl try it on first."

"Oh, no!" said Morgan's messenger, and she tightened her grip on the cloak, lest they compel her to put it on. "This cloak was made for a queen, not a messenger."

But Sir Lancelot stepped forward, snatched the crocodile cloak, and swung it over the young messenger's shoulders.

At once, the cloak burst into flames and the young woman screamed. White tongues of flame, yellow, orange, and bronze!

The more she struggled and the louder she screamed, the tighter the cloak became. As rigid as armor.

The king and queen and their court watched, horrified, as in front of them the young woman was burned alive.

"Merlin," said the king in a quiet voice. "Merlin, where are you?"

But the magician had retreated to the gloom at the back of the hall and seemed to be in a world of his own.

"White must meet black," Merlin intoned. "Let dark fall to light. Let the skylark eat the worm."

What was he talking about?

"Merlin," said Arthur again, but before he could say more, in the deathly stillness of the stone hall, the old enchanter clapped his wrinkled hands, swiped the smoky air, shook his head, and growled, "No! Do not ask me."

"But I need——"

"No!"

"I——"

Merlin shook his head and howled. He howled, and everyone stared at him, astonished. Everyone except

Nimue. She stood quietly beside the magician, her head bowed.

"Ask me not!" cried Merlin. "I am already elsewhere. I am losing my mind."

"Merlin!" the king cried, stepping toward the magician and reaching out with both hands.

"Away!" bellowed the magician, warding him off with his staff. "Away!"

"Merlin!" Arthur cried, and all the desolation of the world was in his cry.

| | | | | | | | | | | | | | | | | | | | | | | | | | | | | | | | | | |

A little way beyond the abbey where the nuns had nursed King Arthur, the land became hilly. Behind the shoulders of each hill was a plunging valley, and then another larger hill. And instead of jostling for space, all the ash trees and beeches and oaks began to thin out and stand apart from one another.

This is where Nimue led Merlin, or Merlin led Nimue, three days after Morgan's messenger had burned to death.

The two of them rode up to a massive overhanging rock, and in its dark shadow, they dismounted. Around them were a tumble of smaller rocks, little runways of scree, and a forest of ferns. The whole place looked tip-tilted and topsy-turvy, as if long ago it had once been a giants' playground.

Merlin had told his apprentice that magic sounds could open a secret way into this rock——through a tunnel and into a cavern——and that there was no way out again, none at all, if the same sounds were repeated by a second person.

Nimue doubted very much that the enchanter would ever teach the words to her. Nervously, she asked him questions about time and memory, how to whip up storms, how to wound and heal, and how to communicate with spirits, and all the while, she was anxious that Merlin would drug her or enchant her. He was so besotted with her that it frightened her.

Was it that Merlin wanted to impress her? Was it that she had simply worn him out with all her questions? Or did Merlin know that he could best help King Arthur

by obliging the king to help himself? A little of each, maybe.

As the two of them stood right in front of the rock, Merlin filled his wheezing lungs, then sighed deeply.

"You know how to enter," breathed Nimue.

Merlin gently nodded. "You can enter anything if you know how."

"You go first," Nimue told him. She so longed to be free of him.

The enchanter looked at her with his old eyes. "Will you come with me?" he asked.

Nimue dipped her head.

Did Merlin know what was going to happen? Well, didn't he always know?

But knowing what's going to happen doesn't mean you can keep it from happening. Merlin murmured the magic sounds.

Nimue listened. She listened and she heard as a wild animal hears.

Slowly, very slowly, the rock opened its jaws, and without another backward look, the enchanter walked in.

At once Nimue sang out the same sounds. The rock shifted and closed its jaws with a grinding sound, trapping Merlin inside.

Nimue watched. For a long time, she waited, and she hadn't the least wish of ever allowing its dark jaws to open again.

||||||||||||||||||||||||||||||||

Some days after Nimue had turned Merlin's own magic against him, King Arthur sat alone at the Round Table, hunched over, his forehead resting on the cool crystal tabletop.

He sat very still. At times he closed his eyes, at times widened them. He saw how the half-moon table was enriched with little golden disks he had never seen before and how the tiny dark tadpoles had swollen and become bloated, and how some of the splits and fissures had widened into threatening gashes. And he knew how the Round Table somehow reflected the minds and hearts of the knights who sat at it, and the health and sickness of his whole kingdom——the kingdom of Britain.

No one at court and no messenger

had told the king what had happened to Merlin, because no one likely even knew. But Arthur knew. His head, his heart, they both knew. His whole body knew.

Like a boy or young man whose father has just died, Arthur felt fragile, yet at the same time all the more responsible for everyone in his care.

With his head still bowed, the king remembered, remembered . . . "We'll slow the hours down if we need to . . . You only accept my advice when it suits you . . . I could find you a wife no less spirited, no less lovely, but I'm warning you, Arthur . . . Whether I'm here or not, time will tell. But I will tell you . . ."

King Arthur sighed, and slowly he sat up.

He and the knights of the Round Table had survived their fourth trial, the trial of magic, by defeating Morgan and her black magic. But he had lost Merlin, who had always been his teacher and his guide.

Just then, a young man with long, scruffy fair hair——aged thirteen, fourteen perhaps——walked straight into the great hall and up to the Round Table.

"Hello!" the young man said to Arthur. "Who are you?"

King Arthur frowned. "Who said you could come in here?"

"I did."

"What do you mean?"

"I said I could. I gave myself permission."

"I see," said Arthur.

"I'm looking for the king. He's called Arthur."

The corners of the king's mouth twitched. "You've found him."

"What do you mean?"

"I am the king. I am King Arthur."

"You are?" exclaimed the young man. "Well, that's a bit of luck."

King Arthur leaned forward and planted his elbows firmly on the table. "Who are you?"

"Mind if I sit down?" the young man asked. "It's been a long hike."

"Sit on that stool there," the king directed.

"All right," the young man said. "Now! You were asking. My name's

Perceval and I come from Wales. My mother and I live in the middle of a pine forest."

"So how . . . ?" began the king. "Why . . . ?"

"Slow down!" the young man said. "Don't spoil my story. A couple of months ago, I was out hunting when five men rode into our forest. They were shining brightly, what with wearing steel all over them. Armor, it's called. They said they were knights and then they told me that King Arthur had made them knights. They were so beautiful and strong, I decided right then that I wanted to be a knight too and was going to find this King Arthur wherever he was. Oh! What a lot of words!"

King Arthur smiled. "Take your time," he said.

"It's been a devil of a journey," the young man went on. "And everything's been so strange since I left the forest."

"Strange?"

"Yes! I found a girl inside a church. At least I thought it was a church because it was that beautiful and my mother says a church is the most beautiful thing there is, but the girl said no, it wasn't a church but a tent. I kissed her seven times, but I don't think she really wanted me to."

"No?" said Arthur, and he shook his head.

"I thought she'd offer me her ring when I'd kissed her, but she didn't, so I took it anyhow, and she snatched it back, and she yelled at me. You see what I mean? Everything's strange."

Arthur raised his right hand. "You were wrong to do that," he said. "Very wrong."

"Anyhow," the young man went on, "I told the girl her skin was so white——as white as snowdrops and mayflowers and apple blossoms and angels' wings——that I was going to call her White Flower. And do you know what she said?"

"What?"

"She said, 'Blanche Fleur. That's my name anyhow. Blanche Fleur.'"

"White Flower, yes," Arthur repeated gravely.

"Anyway," said the young man. "Will you knight me now?"

King Arthur gently shook his head.

"No? Well, could you at least let me sit in this seat? There's no flag or anything hanging over it, so no one would think I was a real knight."

"No," said the king. "That seat is the Perilous Seat."

"Perilous. What does that mean?"

"It's the seat awaiting the knight who achieves the quest of the Holy Grail and——"

"You're talking in riddles," Perceval complained.

"And . . ." Arthur repeated, "who achieves the quest of the Holy Grail and heals the bleeding Fisher King, and cures the Wasteland."

Perceval scratched his head. "What?"

Outside one of the doors of the great hall, there was a noise——the sound of a man singing, and then of clumping feet and little, jingling bells.

"Did you hear that?" said Perceval. "Is it angels?"

King Arthur stood up.

"Is it?"

"No!" exclaimed the king, laughing and growling at the same time. "Not Sir Dagonet again!"

Two long arms waved inside the frame of the hall door, and then a long body appeared behind them, singing:

"A blessing of bells.
A stray of simpletons,
*   hayseeds, and muttonheads.*
A state of grace."

Perceval listened, openmouthed and enchanted.

King Arthur looked at the boy, and he smiled. "Well, now that you've found me . . . you may as well stay. Stay here at Camelot, and learn what's what." | | | | | | | | | | | | | | | | | | | | | | |

VIII

‖ THE QUEST FOR THE HOLY GRAIL ‖

Corbenic and the Fisher King

Merlin was right, King Arthur thought. He told me the time would soon come when I wanted to admit more knights to the fellowship of the Round Table because of their achievements.

So the king summoned carvers and carpenters from the court of King Leodegrance in Cornwall to figure out how the size of the great crystal table could be increased.

They extended it by sawing and fitting two massive semicircular outer tables of oak, each of them more than one foot thick and four feet across. These outer tables surrounded the crystal table, with an opening between them, so that the knights could sit on the inside as well as the outside, facing one another.

There was space at the new table for twenty-four knights.

"It's as if we were being helped," one of the carpenters told King Arthur.

"Yes, what should have taken months took only weeks," said another.

The king was in no doubt, and greatly consoled. He was quite sure that, wherever he was and whatever had befallen him, Merlin had somehow assisted the Cornish carpenters.

It was two years after Nimue had imprisoned Merlin, at the feast preceding Pentecost, that the twelve new knights admitted to the fellowship stepped

forward and dropped onto one knee before Arthur. Each of them repeated the same vows sworn by the first knights admitted to the Round Table and kissed King Arthur's right hand.

Seven trumpeters blew golden notes, and Sir Lucan, the butler of the Round Table, led each new knight to his place, already marked by his banner, and announced, "This is the seat of Sir Breunor. This is the seat of Sir Persides."

One by one by one.

"Sir Alexander.

"Sir Palomides.

"Sir Miles.

"Sir Bors.

"Sir Constantine.

"Sir Agravain.

"Sir Priamus.

"Sir Colgrevaunce."

Last but one, King Arthur admitted Perceval to the Round Table.

"You're still very green," the king told him.

"Green?"

"Innocent. Unproven. But I see you for who you will become. You traveled far from your pine forest in Wales to Camelot, but you've traveled even farther during the last twenty-four months."

And last of all, the king admitted his own son to the Round Table. Mordred knelt in front of his father, and his thick lips twitched. For years, his own mother, Morgause, and his aunt Morgan had poisoned his mind against Arthur. He had grown bitterly jealous of the king. The light in Mordred's eyes masked a darkness in his mind and heart.

Midway through this ceremony, a young woman mounted on a white mule entered the great hall at Camelot. No one had seen her before, and no one knew who she was. When she trotted right up to King Arthur and Queen Guinevere, took a very close look at them, and brayed loudly, most of the knights laughed and brayed too.

"Dismount!" Sir Lucan ordered the stranger.

But the young woman didn't stir. She was wearing a plain white linen wimple. It was not even embroidered with little birds or flowers, let alone inlaid with pearls or diamonds. Around her neck hung a shield, as dazzling white as a field of new-fallen snow lit by the sun. On it were painted two slashes, as scarlet as fresh blood, forming a cross.

"You heard!" Sir Kay called out. "Dismount!"

In answer, the young woman bowed her head to King Arthur. "Forgive me, sire, but I cannot."

"Cannot or will not?" Sir Kay demanded.

"Young woman," said the queen, her voice so low and husky, so beautiful, "when the king is dismounted, we must all dismount."

The young woman drove her feet into her stirrups and stood up in her saddle.

"You knights!" she called out. "You shining knights of the Round Table. You're the finest men in our kingdom of Britain. Some monks claim you're the greatest gathering ever to assemble in one place at one time. And yet all around you, our green land is wilting and going to waste. Our people are suffering. Rich

men are greedy and grasping; poor women and men become even poorer; murderers and robbers roam freely."

King Arthur stood. "My knights and I have sworn to uphold justice in our estates and wherever we go," he replied, "but I know very well there is still great suffering."

"Because of all the cowardice and hatred and sin around you," the young woman said, "the land itself is diseased. Our wells are drying up. Crops fail; apples and pears and plums wither on the branch; not even the berries in the hedgerows ripen. Blackberries, elderberries . . . Our herds of cattle and sheep, even our chickens, are little more than bags of bones. My lord the Fisher King, keeper of the Holy Grail, has been wounded, and the whole world is becoming a wasteland."

The king listened and lowered his eyes.

"Is there no man here," the young woman insisted, "no knight brave enough and blameless enough to ride to Corbenic, the Fisher King's castle?"

The young woman looked around her, and each knight in the great hall felt as if she was seeing straight into his own heart.

"Corbenic!" the young woman repeated. "That's where you'll find the shrine of the Holy Grail, the chalice from which Christ's disciples drank at the Last Supper. That's where the Fisher King lies in terrible agony because of his wounds, as he must always do, until the Grail knight asks the question, the one question that will cure him."

"What is it?" asked King Arthur. "That question."

"That's for you to find out," she replied.

Then the young woman lifted her right hand, and removed her wimple.

The knights gasped.

She was completely bald except for a few gray wisps of hair at the back of her neck.

Then the young woman did dismount. She walked her white mule over to one of the stone pillars in the hall. On the pillar, she hung her white shield with the scarlet cross.

"Here hangs the cross of Christ," she called out, "and here it will remain until one of you achieves the quest of the Holy Grail. Is there not a single man in this kingdom so brave and blameless that he can ride to Corbenic, and ask the question, and return here?"

King Arthur gestured to the one seat always left empty at the Round Table. "This is the seat for the knight who asks that question," he reminded his knights. "The Perilous Seat. We've succeeded in our first four trials—— the trial of friendship and bravery, the trial of love, the trial of honor, and the trial of magic. This is our fifth trial: the quest for the Holy Grail."

||||||||||||||||||||||||||||||||||||||

Many knights at Camelot were stirred and moved by the young woman's woeful appearance and even more by her words. Many vowed to ride to the castle at Corbenic, though they knew they were unlikely to succeed.

"If anyone can cure the Fisher King and heal the Wasteland," King Arthur said, "it will be you, Sir Lancelot. You've proven yourself to be the strongest, the most dauntless, the most manly of us all."

Sir Lancelot bowed his head. "I will quest for the Holy Grail," he vowed, "but not yet."

"Well, I don't like being in another knight's shadow," Sir Gawain declared, impetuous and intrepid as ever. "I'll set off on my own for Corbenic tomorrow."

True to his word, first thing the next day, Sir Gawain rode into the high hills south of Camelot, where one can smell the salt of the sea.

He trotted along a ridge until he came to a stone barrow. When he dismounted, ducked his head, and peered in, he saw an old man sitting in the gloom. It was Nascien the hermit.

"Ah, yes!" said the hermit. "Sir Gawain, I've been expecting you."

"Will you give me your blessing?" Sir Gawain asked. "I'm riding to the castle at Corbenic."

"What for?" demanded the hermit.

"To ask the question."

"You! The same Sir Gawain who beheaded Lady Saraide while hunting the White Stag?"

"By mistake!" the knight protested.

"And didn't Queen Guinevere and her court of ladies sentence you to always guard with your own life any lady who has been wronged?"

Sir Gawain nodded.

"And didn't you accept the gift of the magic girdle from Sir Bertilak's wife, and wrap it around your waist, so as to protect your own miserable life?"

Sir Gawain lowered his head in shame.

"I've heard dozens of stories about you," Nascien told him, "about your resolve and your ambitions. Few of your exploits have been honorable."

"Will you give me your blessing?" the knight repeated quietly. "I'm riding to Corbenic."

The hermit sighed. "Well . . . may God pardon you, Gawain. May God pardon and redeem you, as He pardons and redeems all sinners."

Having secured the hermit's

blessing, Sir Gawain rode west. He was halfway to Cornwall when he reached the castle of Corbenic, and there he crossed nine stone bridges and nine dark moats and found the wounded Fisher King.

The Fisher King's bed was in the open air, beneath a canopy of grape vines, but all the grapes were shriveled. The king was in such pain that he couldn't stop twisting and writhing and groaning.

From the Fisher King, Sir Gawain learned the five words—— the question he must ask when he set eyes on the Holy Grail.

"Remember," the Fisher King groaned.

"I will," Sir Gawain promised him. "I will remember."

Three servants led Sir Gawain to an inner room in Corbenic castle where twelve white-haired men were waiting. With them, he broke bread and sipped red wine, and then the Holy Grail floated into the room. Though covered with stiff white samite, it glowed brightly. Sir Gawain was struck dumb. He opened his mouth and tried to speak, but he couldn't even croak. He tried again but became very hot and breathless, and couldn't remember the question.

Then the Grail floated away, away and out of sight, and Sir Gawain felt tired. So very tired. As if all his efforts and all the wrongs he had done in his life were weighing him down.

He sat on a couch and closed his eyes and fell into a deep sleep. And by the time he woke, he was already mounted on Gringolet and riding back to Camelot.

| | | | | | | | | | | | | | | | | | | | | | | | | | | | | | | | | | | | | | | | | | | | | | | | | | |

After Sir Gawain had ridden out of Camelot to search for the castle of Corbenic and the suffering Fisher King, in the weeks between Pentecost and the summer solstice, many more knights of the Round Table set off in search of the Holy Grail.

More knights are questing than have stayed here at Camelot, King Arthur thought. Some of them will be killed too, or be so badly wounded that they'll never come back. Not only have I lost Merlin, but our great gathering can never, never be the same again.

Many ladies at court said to each other that they had never known the king to be so gloomy.

Sir Lancelot didn't set out to quest for the Grail. Nor did he ride north to attend to his estate at Joyous Gard. Sir Lancelot remained at Camelot. He was so lovestruck by Queen Guinevere that any hour not spent in her company was to him an hour wasted. The strongest and bravest knight in the whole country was drawn again and again to her bright flame.

One June morning, while the king was discussing the planting of new rose bushes with two of his gardeners, a small group of people slowly advanced along the broad gravel path toward him. The group consisted of a gray-haired woman, a younger woman, and a man lying on a litter, carried by servants.

"Your Majesty," the older woman said, "I'm Agatha, and this is my daughter Fyleloly."

"A curious name," said Arthur with a friendly smile.

The older woman gestured to the man on the litter. "And this is her brother, Sir Urry."

"What's wrong with him?" asked the king.

"Seven wounds, sire. Seven! Three open head wounds, three open body wounds, and look—— look at his right hand."

"He's lucky to be alive," said the king.

"Urry is my son," Agatha told him. "He fought and killed Sir Alphegus, but none of us knew Alphegus's mother was a sorceress. She sang spells over my son and told Fyleloly that her brother's wounds would never, never heal unless each one of them was

||171||

touched by the greatest strength."

"Ah!" said the king, turning to his gardeners. "The greatest strength. Summer sunlight. The magic touch of soft rain."

"No!" said Agatha. "Touched by the strength of the greatest knight in the world. My daughter and I have crossed the Alpine mountains. We've crossed the whole of Europe and searched for seven years for that man."

"My lady," King Arthur said to her, "we're not magicians and we're not healers. But there are certainly some strong men here. Maybe one will be stronger than the spells cast by Sir Alphegus's mother."

King Arthur summoned all the knights still at Camelot to meet him and the queen and Agatha and her daughter the next morning in the castle gardens. Again the day was bright, sweetened by night rain. The white lilac had not yet withered and swam in its own thick scent, and the crumpled purple irises exuded their dark, mysterious perfume.

"A day for healing," the king told Agatha. "A day for growing. Have faith, now!"

The old woman crossed her breast. Then servants laid two cushions on the grass beside the gravel path, and she and Fyleloly knelt on them.

"I'll touch your son's wounds myself," the king told her. "If God wills it, I'll succeed. If not, one of my knights will want to try."

Then Arthur bent over Sir Urry, lying on his litter. He opened both his hands and gently laid them over two of the knight's wounds——one that had exposed the tendons on his left shoulder and one that had mangled his right hand and nearly severed it from the wrist.

At once, both wounds began to pulse, as if they were strange creatures with lives of their own. Within a few seconds, as Queen Guinevere and everyone watched, they began to bleed. The blood streamed down Sir Urry's left arm.

King Arthur pursed his lips and shook his head, dismayed that his touch seemed to make the wounds worse.

Then several of the Round Table

knights followed the king and laid their hands on Sir Urry's open, sticky wounds.

"I feel so weak," the knight murmured. "Yet I can feel the strength of your care and concern."

The king looked around at his knights. "Where's Lancelot?" he asked.

And almost as if he had heard him, Sir Lancelot, Arthur's greatest knight, walked down the castle steps into the gardens, and there the king told him how the wounded knight could be healed.

"Not I, sire," said Sir Lancelot. "If none of my companions here can heal this poor man . . ."

King Arthur looked around at his circle of knights. "Understand," he told them, "that we are one fellowship. One unbroken circle. We remain equals whether or not Sir Lancelot succeeds."

Still Sir Lancelot demurred.

"I command you," the king said to him.

Sir Lancelot glanced at Queen Guinevere.

Guinevere returned his gaze. "Lancelot!" she breathed, and her breath was the scent of honeysuckle. "Lancelot!"

Sir Lancelot bowed his head in prayer, then opened his hands and laid them on two of Sir Urry's wounds. He laid them on two more. He laid them on seven. And one by one the open wounds began to darken a little. They closed, and blood clotted over them, and scars sealed them.

All the knights in the garden got down on their knees. Some were astonished, some admiring, some jealous. And many of them heard in their hearts the words of the young woman after she had hung her shield on a pillar in the great hall and demanded whether one of them would be brave enough and blameless enough to ask the right question at the castle of Corbenic.

"Let us all praise God and give thanks," said King Arthur.

Sir Urry sat up. He stretched out his hands and arms and embraced the sweet summer morning.

||||||||||||||||||||||||||||||||

After Lancelot healed Sir Urry's seven wounds, the summer passed with stifling slowness. The days would not let go of their intense heat, and the evenings and nights were hot.

Wearing nothing but her ivory silk shift, her blazing red-gold hair uncombed and unrestrained, Guinevere lay on her bed, unable to sleep and listening to the little night sounds——the crick and crack of roof tiles, slightly cooling now, the fitful buzzing of a dopy fly, the tremulous hoot of a tawny owl.

Then there was a peck at her little barred window.

A nightingale, was it? Surprised at its own reflection?

Another peck.

Guinevere got up from her bed, stepped to her window, and looked out. Standing below her window, flooded in moonlight, was Sir Lancelot.

"Lancelot!" she gasped.

"My lady," said Sir Lancelot in a hoarse voice. "I had to see you." Then he dropped a pebble from his right hand.

The queen smiled. She shivered.

"Throwing pebbles, were you?" she teased. "Like a little boy."

"My lady," said Sir Lancelot, "shall I come up?"

The queen shivered again. "Come up? You can fly, then, can you?"

"I have a ladder."

"Ladder!"

"From the orchard. For picking high fruit."

Guinevere felt quite breathless. "You think I'm an apple?"

"My lady, I think you're a temptation!"

Again, the owl hooted. Its trembling call seemed to come from all around them.

"Shall I come up?" Sir Lancelot asked again.

The queen didn't reply.

"Your silence," said the knight. "It doesn't mean no."

"It doesn't mean yes," Guinevere replied.

"Without courage," said Sir Lancelot, " a man's no better than a chicken."

Lancelot positioned the wooden

ladder against the wall and rapidly climbed it. He gripped two of the iron bars guarding her window and wrenched them right out of the stone. He grabbed a third bar with his left hand and tugged it, squeezed it, but then it snapped in his hand. It cut his hand to the bone.

With a gasp, Lancelot stumbled through the little window into the queen's bedroom. There he stood, sword in hand, dripping blood, in front of Guinevere.

At once the queen tore a strip from the hem of her silk shift and wrapped it around Sir Lancelot's bloodstained hand.

"A deep wound," she said.

Sir Lancelot smiled and placed his right hand over his heart. "Very deep," he replied.

Queen Guinevere took her knight's hand and placed it gently over her own heart, and her knight could feel it hammering. Hammering.

"I love you," Sir Lancelot said.

How to describe the way a woman and a man feel when they know they're in love? It is a kind of sickness, a joyful illness in which you can scarcely think of anything else. It's a hot-and-cold fever. It is the most fearful and playful and painful and precious and tender and forceful and holy feeling in the world.

Queen Guinevere took Sir Lancelot into her warm arms.

The moon, buttercup and bruised, watched them.

"I know we are breaking sacred rules," Sir Lancelot said, "yet I do not feel that what we are doing is shameful."

"I love you," Guinevere whispered. "But for all the world, I do not wish to hurt my husband nor shame my king. So no one must know."

"A knight should fear shame more than his own death," said Sir Lancelot. "Armed with your love, I will quest for the Holy Grail. At the castle of Corbenic, I will ask the question."

| | | | | | | | | | | | | | | | | | | | | | | | | | | | | | | | | | | |

The old hermit Nascien scarcely had a day to himself.

Following Sir Gawain's example, many more knights of the Round Table visited Nascien in his stone barrow, and he enabled each to better understand his own faults but failed to dissuade any from continuing his quest.

"Well, Sir Lancelot," Nascien said, "I suppose you've come to make your confession too."

"I have."

"And you'll confess all your sins?"

"I will," the knight replied, and he got down on his knees.

"And faithfully swear never to repeat them?"

Sir Lancelot stared at the ground and sighed.

"And faithfully swear never to repeat them," the hermit said again.

"Yes," Sir Lancelot said quietly. "Except one."

Nascien waited.

The knight sighed again. "The lady I love is another man's wife."

"Queen Guinevere!" the hermit rasped.

Sir Lancelot looked up at him, startled. "No," he said. "Yes."

"You fool!"

"I've never said a word, not to anyone. Neither has she. I've never shamed my king."

Nascien growled. "I've heard about all your great deeds. I know you have no rival. But you're blind, Lancelot. You're Judas. You're crucifying Jesus."

Sir Lancelot shook his head. "I can confess our love," he said, "but I can never regret it. How can I ever regret anything so pure, so unstained? So honorable?"

"So honorable! Your feelings—— they're not love. They're infatuation."

"No!" the knight exclaimed.

"You're blind!" the hermit told him again. "If you don't regret them, will you nevertheless promise to set your feelings aside? Will you vow to put them all behind you?"

Again Sir Lancelot stared at the dusty ground, and then he stared through the gloom at the old hermit.

"I promise," he said.

||||||||||||||||||||||||||||||||||||||||||

Sir Blamore . . .
    Sir Dinas . . .
    Sir Galahantine . . .
    Sir Owain . . .
    Sir Marc . . .
    Sir Partinel . . .
    Sir Fergus . . .

A litany of knights had quested for the Grail after Sir Gawain and before Sir Lancelot, and not one of them had been able to cross the nine bridges and nine dark moats and enter into the castle at Corbenic.

But then came Sir Lancelot. He walked across the withered grass to the little open pavilion where the wounded Fisher King lay on his bed and knelt beside him. And there he saw and heard a wimpled woman singing. Was it the same young woman who had ridden to Camelot on a white mule and challenged all the knights of the Round Table? Sir Lancelot wasn't sure. And he couldn't make sense of the words of her song, simple as they were:

"The falcon has carried
    my mate away.
He carried him up,
    he carried him down.
He carried him into
    an orchard brown . . ."

Was the brown orchard the same as the withered grass and the wasteland around them? Sir Lancelot wondered. Was it the same as our wilting green world? And who was the mate? Was he the wounded Fisher King? And if so, who was the falcon?

"Beside that bed a young
    woman stays,
And she sobs by night and day . . ."

Sir Lancelot knew that only the Fisher King could tell him the

question he had to ask when he set eyes on the Holy Grail, but he was still puzzling over the young woman's song, and when the Fisher King whispered the five words of the question, Lancelot failed to hear them fully.

Then the king writhed and yelled because of his pain. He gasped and, despite Sir Lancelot's entreaties, was unable to repeat the words.

Just like Sir Gawain before him, Lancelot was next conducted to the room where twelve white-haired men awaited him, and there he broke bread and sipped red wine with them. But when the Holy Grail floated into the room, still covered in stiff white samite, and again the whole room glowed, Sir Lancelot didn't even see it.

He was blind to it.

For him, it was not there.

Sir Lancelot slept on the same couch where Sir Gawain had slept, and when at last he woke, he was already riding straight back to Camelot and into the warm arms of Queen Guinevere.

At times on his journey back, Lancelot was heavy-hearted. Maybe I'm stronger than any other knight, he thought, maybe more brave, but I've failed my king. I've failed in our quest for the Holy Grail.

At other times, he was almost light-hearted. He knew Guinevere would be waiting for him. It's only because I love her so deeply, he said to himself, it's only because of my passion for her that I failed to remember the question. I failed as any man is bound to fail, because he's a man!

||||||||||||||||||||||||||||||||||||||

From near and far and from across the sea, knights set off to find the castle of Corbenic, to seek the Holy Grail, and to heal the Fisher King. Some were gone for twelve months, some even longer.

Sir Galelot . . .
Sir Lionel . . .
Sir Loholt . . .
Sir Sagremor . . .
Sir Brandeliz . . .
The Black Knight . . .

Sir Priamus of Tuscany . . .

Three knights——strangers to one another——each riding on his own, drew near to Corbenic at the end of June, the month when half the world should be swathed in roses of every color. But the nearer they drew to the castle, the more afflicted the natural world around them became. The roses were cankered. Leaves on the fruit trees were curled and brittle; tall silver birches leaned over sideways, as if weary of life.

Although the knights were unknown to one another, they had much in common. Each man practiced what he preached, unlike so many of their fellow knights. Each upheld the highest ideals. And during his quest, each had seen marvels and accomplished great feats.

Sir Bors was rather like his name. Direct and straightforward. He was an honest, kind man from the Yorkshire Moors. He ate plain food and talked plain talk and had little time for men who put on airs and used elaborate and unnecessarily long words.

"I'm a common or garden knight," he sometimes said, and he was double the age of Sir Perceval.

Sir Perceval!

Well, although more than two years had passed since he had arrived from North Wales and invited himself into Camelot, he was still as innocent as a daisy.

King Arthur could see Perceval's strength of mind and his sweet purity of heart, and the way in which the world's wrongs and sorrows didn't quell his hopefulness——the way in which he wanted to trust everyone——and that was why he had knighted him and admitted him to the fellowship of the Round Table.

"My whole life's a wonder journey," Sir Perceval said, opening his arms. "A Wunderreise."

And Sir Galahad! He was Sir Lancelot's own son, and younger than Sir Bors. His mother was Amite, the daughter of King Pelles. After drinking a potion, Sir Lancelot had made love to her believing he was making love to Queen Guinevere. This was many years

before he and the queen had embarked on their relationship. Galahad was so strong, so skilled and handsome, and yet so innocent that he had never even kissed a girl.

Between them and each on his own, these three knights had been to the Revolving Castle that never stopped turning, had fought lions and bears, rescued ladies woefully and wrongfully imprisoned, and killed the giant called the Knight of the Dragon, whose shield was embossed with a dragon's head that spurt fire and foul-smelling smoke. They had talked to sorcerers and quested for lost words——words to turn into spells and to help heal the Wasteland. They had sat at firesides and marveled when they learned the names of ancient Welsh warriors:

Flamelord . . .

Hundred Claws . . .

Son of Seventh . . .

Mighty Thigh . . .

Angel Face . . .

Little Son of Three Cries . . .

Someone . . .

Each of their names also had a meaning, the three knights learned. Bors, Perceval, and Galahad: fight, Pierce the Valley, and Hawk. Its own music and meaning. And each knight must grow into his own bright name.

Side by side, Sir Bors and Sir Perceval and Sir Galahad crossed the nine bridges and the dark moats where monstrous diseased carp glided silently beneath rotten lily pads.

They took off their helmets and laid down their swords. Together they crossed the jaundiced grass and knelt at the bedside of the Fisher King.

Like Sir Lancelot, they saw the wimpled young woman. And when she began to sing, her words were somehow in their hearts and on their tongues. Although they had never heard her song before, they were at once able to join in.

The old world, with all its busyness, distractions, causes, and confusions, was a world away. Their quest was behind them. They were faithful and unflinching, intent and very, very strong. With the young woman, they sang:

"And in that bed there was a knight,
His wounds bleeding day and night.
Beside that bed a young woman stays,
And she sobs by night and day.
And beside that bed there
     stands a stone,
Corpus Christi engraved thereon."

In the silence following the song, the three knights came to understand in their hearts that the Fisher King was Jesus's disciple on earth. They understood what wrong we do each time we hurt one another or damage the earth we all share.

Their eyes shone. Their cheeks were wet with tears.

Then the Fisher King entrusted them with the question, the five words to ask when they set eyes on the Holy Grail.

"It's within your power to heal the Wasteland," he told them. "Indeed, it's within the power of every person to do so. But you three men are the chosen ones."

The Fisher King shuddered and doubled over at the pain in his gut. "I've waited so very long for you," he croaked.

"Go now. Go straight to the Chapel of the Grail, and when the time comes, ask the question."

The wimpled young woman accompanied the three knights to the chapel. There the twelve white-haired men were waiting for them, and then, right in front of them, the Holy Grail floated in. It hung in midair, so close to them that they could see their own reflections in it. And it was made not of metal or wood or any kind of matter but entirely of light . . .

"Vas spirituale," the wimpled woman whispered. "The spiritual vessel." And after a while, she continued, "The Holy Grail is Mary, the mother of Jesus, and Mary is the Holy Grail. Within her lies the body of Christ and the blood of Christ."

The three knights bowed their heads.

"Female and male," the young woman whispered. "The Grail is both."

When they raised their heads, the knights saw the figure of a man, wearing a loincloth, rising from the Grail.

"My sons!" said the man. "My three sons!"

The three knights trembled.

Sir Bors and Sir Perceval and Sir Galahad remembered to ask the question the Fisher King had entrusted to them.

"Whom does the Grail feed?" they asked in unison.

"She feeds me," said the man, "and I feed you. Each of you is a vessel too. Each child and woman and man on earth can become a grail, a vessel brimming with holy spirit."

The man then raised his head and eyes, and raised his arms and hands. In a beam brighter than sunlight, He rose above the Grail. He ascended into heaven.

|||||||||||||||||||||||||||||||||||||||||||||||||||||||||||||||||||

That day of days, each of the three knights walked alone in the meadows and woods surrounding the castle of Corbenic.

Each felt as if time did not exist, yet each could recall all that had happened in his life, and on that day, and could also foresee events that would happen in time yet to come.

They knew there would always be things that cannot be understood until a person is ready to understand them, and that some things cannot be heard until someone is ready to hear them.

"Because of you three knights," the wimpled young woman told them in the cool of the evening, "the Wasteland can grow again. Our Fisher King can at last die peacefully and lie in his grave. You, Perceval, must take his place. You will become our Keeper of the Grail, our new Fisher King."

"I will go on Crusade," said Sir Bors. "I will fight to regain Jerusalem."

"I will first return to Camelot," Sir Galahad said. "I long to tell the king how three of his knights have achieved this great trial——this quest for the Holy Grail. It will fill him with pride, and restore his joy in his kingship. I'm eager, too, to hear all that has happened during our long absence. I will claim the shield hanging on the pillar——the white shield painted with a scarlet cross——and I'll take my place in the Perilous Seat. Then I will be ready to die."

"Wherever you go in this wide world," the young woman warned them, "remember what you've sworn as knights of the Round Table. Remember how so many men are jealous and worse, bitter and worse, crooked and worse, greedy and worse, violent and worse, vengeful and worse. You must do everything you possibly can so that each knight becomes as you have become."

Then the young woman swept back her linen wimple. And the three knights saw that she was bald no longer. Her beautiful fair hair was growing again. ||||||||||||

IX

|| THE TRIAL OF LOVE AND LOYALTY ||

SIR LANCELOT AND QUEEN GUINEVERE

Three years.

Sir Galahad had taken his place in the Perilous Seat. Sir Bors had gone on Crusade and was fighting to regain Jerusalem. Sir Perceval had become the new Keeper of the Grail, the new Fisher King.

Three long years had passed since Sir Lancelot had last entered the cold stone cloister at Camelot. Standing in the shadows, he watched King Arthur lead a procession of knights and their ladies out of the castle chapel.

The king, though not old, walked with a slight stoop, as if he were carrying a heavy load on his back, and his tread looked weary.

Sir Lancelot stared, and he ached.

The last person to step out of the chapel, just when Sir Lancelot had supposed she might not have come to the evening service at all, was Queen Guinevere.

As soon as the king and his retinue had left the cloisters, Sir Lancelot stepped from the shadows and strode toward her.

Guinevere saw him, and hesitated. She covered her mouth with her right hand and lowered her eyes.

And then Lancelot was standing right in front of her.

She raised her head, and their eyes met. At once, the knight could see how

her cheeks had hollowed and how she looked almost wounded, and yet how beautiful she was.

"Lancelot," she said softly.

Lancelot longed to step forward and sweep her into his arms. But when is life ever as easy as that? He was cautious; he was wary.

"Guinevere," he said. "My Guinevere."

The queen took a deep breath. "Your Guinevere! Your Guinevere, am I?"

"My Guinevere," Lancelot quietly repeated.

"Don't talk to me in that voice," Guinevere said. "Don't! If Merlin were here, he'd tell us that the sixth trial of the knights of the Round Table is our trial too——the trial of love and loyalty. Your loyalty to me, and ours to the king. And I'd tell Merlin that you, Sir Lancelot, have already failed it."

"My lady . . ."

"No! I'm not your lady. No!"

"But . . ."

"Three years! Three years, Lancelot, since you climbed up that ladder. And not once did you send me a single

word. Not once did you send me a secret love token: a tassel, a comb, a mirror, a breastpin."

"Only because——"

"No! Next, you'll protest your innocence."

The queen's voice was rising and carried into every corner of the cloister.

"Knights here," she went on, "have informed me how you flirted on your way home."

"No."

"Yes! You let a poor sweet girl believe you loved her, and after you left her, she took her own life."

Sir Lancelot stood his ground but lowered his head.

"You don't love me," Queen Guinevere accused him.

"My lady, I do."

"Not as you did three years ago."

"May I speak, my lady?"

"Love is wild and dangerous, almost impossible to control. It's a passion, a wildfire, a furnace. For you, our love's just a memory. It's not love at all."

Queen Guinevere trembled and wept.

Sir Lancelot took the queen gently in his arms. She tried to push him away, but the knight only drew her to him more tightly.

"I know this," he said quietly. "I've never felt such love for any woman as I feel for you, and I've never been loved by any woman as I've been loved by you. Every man in this world would marvel at the power of your love, and I believe each man would know himself incapable of loving with such fervor."

"As I love," Guinevere said between sobs, "all women can love. Each and every woman can love."

"I am your knight, and I love you," Sir Lancelot said. "I love you as much as I always have, and I'll prove it."

Then he held her at arm's length and shouted in a voice so loud that even the earthworms deep in the soil and the larks high in the blue sky could hear him, "I love you, Guinevere! I love you!"

"Shhh!" the queen protested, pressing her soft fingertips to his mouth.

Too late! Much too late. Sir Agravain had already walked into the peaceful cloister; he had already witnessed Queen Guinevere and Sir Lancelot together. And he had already overheard much of what they had said to each other.

|||||||||||||||||||||||||||||||||||||

Sir Agravain was strong. Very strong. And many of the knights of the Round Table were wary of offending him. He was quick to speak his mind, his tongue was caustic, and he was often able to convince others that he was in the right.

He well knew that his sharp thoughts and feelings were often unworthy of an honorable man—— and yet they welled up within him. They fed on one another, and they preyed on him.

Above all, he resented the way he could never match Sir Lancelot, however hard he tried. Sir Lancelot had won more jousts and more tournaments and had been on more quests, and while Sir Agravain sought praise, Sir Lancelot always made light of it. Though Sir Agravain did his best to

conceal it, what had begun as jealousy festered over the months into freezing hatred.

But now! Now that he had actually seen the queen and Sir Lancelot alone together and overheard what they said, especially Lancelot bellowing how he loved her . . . Sir Agravain told himself that he was indignant for his king. The truth was, he was so full of venom and so self-serving that he was prepared to split and shatter the Round Table by telling the king about what he had seen and heard.

Sir Agravain backed out of the cloister, and during the next days, he watched Sir Lancelot and Queen Guinevere like a predatory hawk. He saw how, despite her first fury, Guinevere had almost forgiven Lancelot. He was certain that they would soon become lovers again.

Sir Agravain went to the rooms of his brothers in arms, Gaheris and Gareth, and told them what he had seen and heard. While he was telling them, first Sir Gawain and then Sir

Mordred, the son of King Arthur and Morgause, strode in.

"You're worse than a slug," Sir Gawain told Sir Agravain, "leaving trails of slime behind you. It's none of your business."

"It is my business," retorted Sir Agravain. "It's your business. It's the business of every honorable man at court."

"The king knows nothing of it," Sir Gawain replied, "nothing. If no one speaks of it, no one will be hurt, and it will be as if it hadn't happened."

"You, Sir Gawain," said Sir Agravain, "you're just turning your back on it."

Sir Gawain swatted him away, as if he were a buzzing wasp. "Yes, I am," he said. "I'm turning my back on it. And turning my back on you, Agravain. I won't hear one word more."

With that, Sir Gawain walked away, and the two brothers walked on either side of him.

Sir Mordred looked at Sir Agravain, his eyes black as jet.

"They're all weak-minded," Sir Agravain said. He puffed out his cheeks and blew in the direction of the three men, as if he could scatter and dismiss them like thistledown. "Spineless!"

"So . . ." Sir Mordred prompted him. "We'll tell the king."

Sir Mordred nodded. "We will," he said. And he smiled.

But when Sir Agravain told King Arthur what he had seen and heard in the cloister, and Sir Mordred added that he was quite sure the queen and Sir Lancelot had been lovers in the past, and would become lovers again, the king wouldn't believe them. Or wouldn't permit himself to believe them?

"Never!" he said. "It's right and proper that Lancelot should pay court to her, and I know how much she cares for him. But he's the most honorable of all men. He would never shame me or disgrace the Round Table."

Sir Agravain looked at his feet and scuffed the ground. Then he gave a deep sigh.

"No!" said King Arthur. "Never! Not unless you bring me proof."

Sir Agravain sighed again, and shook his head from side to side as if finding such proof. "I will bring it, then," he said.

One early afternoon, not long after the king and his court moved north to Carlisle, as they did each year, Queen Guinevere and her knight Lancelot prepared to go out hunting together, just the two of them. Sir Lancelot was unarmed except for his sword and his bow and a quiver of arrows.

But Sir Agravain had been watching them and waiting for just such an opportunity. And he persuaded a band of other knights, all fully armed, to help him stalk them.

It grew late. What light there was became dreary, almost lifeless, and the soaring oaks and elms closed around Guinevere and Lancelot. They knew then that they'd be unable to find their way through the dark back to the castle. They had little choice

but to stay in one of the king's small wooden hunting lodges.

The long grass in the glade surrounding the lodge was already dewy. A stand of oxeye daisies shone weakly in the gloom.

Some distance away, Sir Agravain and his companions dismounted. They waited a while, until they thought that Guinevere and Lancelot had likely retired to bed, then quietly approached the lodge. Now and then a metal neck flap clinked or a knee joint creaked, but no louder than the whistle or chirp of some night-bird.

And then? Then they were upon the lodge. Sir Agravain stepped up to the door and pounded the pommel of his sword against it.

Sir Lancelot sat up.

Queen Guinevere threw her arms around the knight's waist. "What's that? What was it?"

"Not a night bird," said Sir Lancelot grimly, and he reached for his sword, which was lying across the foot of the bed.

"You traitors!" bawled a voice outside the hunting lodge.

Sir Lancelot and Queen Guinevere said nothing.

"You traitors! Come out and we'll spare your lives."

Sir Lancelot gave a deep sigh. "My lady," he said.

"Your Guinevere," whispered the queen.

"No thigh plate, no mail shirt, no helmet. I've nothing except for my sword."

"Sweet Lancelot," murmured Guinevere, kissing his right arm, his shoulder, his neck, his cheek.

"Now I'm armed!" Sir Lancelot growled, and he leaped up. "There's nothing for it."

He unbolted the lodge door and opened it a crack. A little more . . . then just a little more, and a knight lowered his head and looked in.

"Welcome!" exclaimed Sir Lancelot, thwacking the man on the side of his head and poleaxing him.

Then he hauled the knight's body

into the lodge and slammed and bolted the door again. The queen stripped the unfortunate man of his armor as quickly as she could, and with it Sir Lancelot armed himself.

"Sir Colgrevaunce," said Sir Lancelot, shaking his head and groaning. "Alas! Not a bad bone in his body. He was never a leader, though. Always a follower."

"May he rest in peace," Guinevere said.

"Now, then!" roared Sir Lancelot, and he unbolted the little door and leaped out. "Who's next?"

Imagine a ferocious bear glaring and snarling, baring its claws, baring its teeth, and springing at a pack of yelping hounds.

Night birds and day birds screamed and whistled and squawked, deer and hares and rabbits dived for cover, and Sir Lancelot set about his foes. He wounded and killed no fewer than twelve of the knights who had followed him and Queen Guinevere into the forest. He even killed Sir Agravain. Only Sir Mordred, King Arthur's own son, escaped.

The queen led a gasping Lancelot back into the lodge. Piece by piece, she took off his armor.

For a while, the knight said nothing. Nothing. And when at last he did so, his voice was choked with sobs. "For all the world, I never imagined fighting and killing a single one of my own companions. So many fine men. Sir Agravain must have plotted this and persuaded the others to go along. There'll be no place for him in heaven."

"You must ride east," Guinevere told him. "Ride to Joyous Gard. Before daylight, you must put miles and miles between yourself and the king and his court."

"*I* must?" Sir Lancelot exclaimed. "No, Guinevere! You and I. Together."

Guinevere shook her head fiercely. "No! I can't! I must stay with the king."

"Never!"

"My place is beside my king. But you, Lancelot . . . As soon as it becomes known what has happened, many knights will follow and support you."

Sir Lancelot buried his face in his

hands and shuddered. "Maybe, yes. Yes, it's true. But Guinevere, my love, my only Guinevere, you can be sure that I'll protect you. No matter what, I'll save you from any threat or harm."

"Go now," sobbed the queen, so tearful, so very rightly fearful. "May God go with you, Lancelot."

||||||||||||||||||||||||||||||||||||||

"We trapped them," Sir Mordred exclaimed, his eyes as wide as black saucers. "Trapped!"

King Arthur closed his eyes.

"In bed. In a hunting lodge. And Lancelot killed twelve men. Twelve."

The king felt weary, so desperately tired.

"Sir Agravain and Sir Colgrevaunce and . . ."

Arthur covered his ears. So tired. So troubled. Somehow he felt far more sickened by Mordred and Sir Agravain than by his own wife, Guinevere, or by Sir Lancelot.

He kept wishing Merlin were there beside him, helping him, advising him. Not for the first time, he heard the magician warning him about how capricious and faithless Guinevere would turn out to be.

"Go away, Mordred!" he growled, and he buried his face in his arms. "Go away!"

His wife had betrayed him; his greatest knight had shamed him; the brazen way in which his own son had informed him utterly disgusted him; and twelve of his knights lay under their shields in the forest. What was Arthur to do?

The king knew he had no choice. According to the law of the land, he would have to do what he could not bear to do. He was obliged to sentence his own wife to be burned to death.

King Arthur laid his forehead on the cool crystal of the Round Table and closed his eyes. When he opened them again, and stared down into the crystal, he could see it was so bruised, so riven and fractured, that it was a wonder it hadn't already split into two. The king knew that nothing now could ever mend it, or ever heal his own heart. His knights could attempt quests almost impossible, and it was true that Sir Galahad, Sir Bors, and Sir Perceval had even achieved the quest of the Holy Grail itself and had been vouchsafed the very greatest of all gifts——that the wasteland of our world would grow green again. But except for those three, King Arthur knew that his knights, even the very best of them, were not saints but flawed, mortal men.

Is this what it is to be human? The king wondered. To be able to dream the greatest and the most golden dream and yet to know that in the end it must fail?

For a long while, the king lay inert, his head still resting on the table. But then he was roused by a familiar sing-song voice. "I'm here. I'm here."

King Arthur opened one eye but could see no one.

The king frowned. "Sir Dagonet. My jester. Where are you?"

"Can't you see me? Merlin's apprentice, Nimue, has used her magic and taken away my body."

King Arthur groaned.

"I accused her of doing away with Merlin," said Sir Dagonet, "and she raged at me. She's taken my body away for a year and a day, but I'll still be here, my king, whether you know it or not. I'll always be close by to hearten and console you, even to make you laugh."

||||||||||||||||||||||||||||||||||||

Once the king laid eyes on the corpses of twelve of his knights and stood beside their graves, he could doubt no longer that Sir Lancelot had shamed him and the Round Table and that his own wife, Guinevere, had betrayed him.

His expression was grim and determined, and his voice was steady as he instructed his servants to hammer a stake into the ground in the wild meadow and build a mound of dead branches around it.

Since this is what must happen, he said to himself, better it were done quickly.

Then he summoned Sir Gawain.

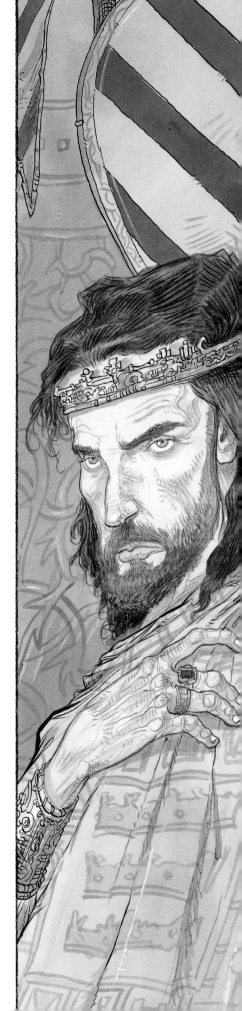

"Arm yourself and have Gaheris and Gareth arm themselves too."

Sir Gawain frowned. "Arm ourselves?"

"And have your squires polish your armor." The king's words caught in his throat. "Nothing but the best."

"Sire?"

"Guinevere," he choked. All at once, the king's eyes flooded with tears. "She must burn."

"No!" exclaimed Sir Gawain.

"The king's wife is not above the law. And if she is allowed to break the law," said King Arthur, "why shouldn't other people break it too? She is guilty of treason."

There was a horsefly buzzing around the two of them, and it settled on Sir Gawain's hand. The knight slapped and killed it, and its blood stained his knuckles.

"Arm yourselves," the king repeated. "Then go to Guinevere's chamber. Bring her to the fire."

"No!" Sir Gawain said. "I will not."

"I'm ordering you."

"I will not, sire. I cannot." Sir Gawain hesitated. "I cannot . . . Sire, she loves you. She's true to you. She has been misled."

"Tell your brothers in arms, then," the king ordered in a stony voice. "Tell them to bring her."

And so it was. On a sweet afternoon, with lamb clouds and light wind from the south-west, Queen Guinevere was brought to the pyre by Sir Gareth and Sir Gaheris. The wind played in her loose red-gold hair. She was wearing a silvery-white linen smock, the color of barley when it just begins to ripen.

People were gathering from all sides in the wild meadow at Carlisle. The whole court: all the knights and their squires and ladies; Lady Maledisant, Sir Breunor's wife; Lady Lyonesse, the wife of Sir Gareth; her sister Lynette;

Lady Laudine; and Nimue's cousin, Lady Lunette. Not only these, but also the armorers, the butchers, children, and dairymaids and fletchers and gravediggers and herdsmen——the whole community of the great border castle at Carlisle.

At first the crowd was simply curious, but when they saw the mound of brushwood and the stake at the heart of it, all fell silent. Guinevere was tied to that stake.

Unblinking, the queen looked straight at the king. So bold. So noble.

King Arthur stared at his queen. He stared and then he began to tremble. He lowered his head, almost overcome with doubt, and love, and pain, and duty.

The whole court, everyone there in that wild meadow, stood very still. Even the light wind held its breath.

The king gave a barely perceptible nod, and the fire was lit.

At first it was slow to take, as if reluctant to do anything so outrageous as burn a beautiful woman. But then the wind breathed on the dead twigs and branches, and wicked tongues began to lick around the queen, and she and her pyre were cocooned in gray smoke.

The wind became uneven. It shredded the ball of smoke and dispersed it to left and right and upward and even downward, but even as it did so, the fire smoked more eagerly, and Queen Guinevere was in the middle of it, writhing.

This is when everyone heard not crying or shrieking, not wailing or screaming, but pounding, pounding, pounding ...

| | | | | | | | | | | | | | | | | | | | | | | | | | | | | | | | | | | |

Sir Lancelot and his followers gallop into the meadow, into the smoke, and lay about them. They cut down armed men, unarmed men, women, children, old

men, young men as if they're harvesting them. And where the smoke is thickest, Sir Lancelot kills Sir Gaheris, then Sir Gareth, both of them unarmed, without even recognizing who they are.

And then Sir Lancelot draws his dagger. He wades into the flames and cuts Guinevere loose.

Sir Lancelot picks her up, light as an armful of feathers. He staggers out of the fire, remounts, and lifts up the queen in front of him.

All around them, there was shouting, choking, bawling, yelling, wailing.

But Sir Lancelot and Queen Guinevere hear nothing of this hubbub. The knight spurs his horse through the cruel, sweet smoke, and away they gallop out of the scorched meadow.

Away!

||||||||||||||||||||||||||||||||

For day upon day in the court at Carlisle, there was a kind of shocked silence. It was as if a damper or muffler had been laid over all the usual sounds——courtiers coming

and going, servants calling and running down passageways, the babble of voices in the great hall. As much as they could, the knights and their ladies and the squires and the whole household avoided the king and his nephew Sir Gawain.

In his fury and distress at the loss of his brothers in arms, Sir Gawain had begun to mutter to himself. He became more and more enraged, more and more embittered, and determined to take revenge against Sir Lancelot for the death of his brothers in arms. As for the king, he became more withdrawn, more silent, more troubled.

It was the same at Joyous Gard. Sir Lancelot's castle seemed bleak and empty. The flint-gray waves of the North Sea pounded and thundered at its walls day after day. Joyous Gard! The name itself mocked the two lovers.

"It's so stony here, and sorrowful," Guinevere complained. "So unwelcoming."

"Our sorrow is in our own hearts," Sir Lancelot said. "It's not the fault of the place."

Alone together, and safe, Queen Guinevere and Sir Lancelot had strangely little to say to each other. For much of the time, they were silent. Each realized that what had happened in the hunting lodge, and then in the wild meadow, had not only destroyed the Round Table but had also changed their love forever. It was not that they didn't still love each other. They did. But their hearts had been hollowed out by all that had happened.

Very often Guinevere thought of the first months of her marriage as if they were a far-off, sunlit country. Then she thought of how she'd been unable to save Arthur from such terrible shame, no matter how much she'd wanted to do so. She thought she'd have done better to burn in the flames.

And very often Sir Lancelot thought

about all the men he had killed at the hunting lodge: that young knight, Priamus, no more than a boy, only just arrived at court, who scarcely spoke English, and the knight from Hungary who had escaped the ring of iron in his own country, and a Welsh lad almost as innocent as Sir Perceval, each of them eager to make his mark and serve the king, all of them so impressionable and all persuaded by Sir Agravain.

When messengers arrived from Carlisle and informed Sir Lancelot that he had cut down Sir Gareth and Sir Gaheris in the smoke of the pyre, he was almost inconsolable. He knew that not only had he forfeited the friendship of the king but that he had also incurred the enmity of his nephew.

"Humans have heads and hearts," he told Guinevere, "and we're able to forgive. Some things, most things, can be forgiven. But a few cannot."

| | | | | | | | | | | | | | | | | | | | | | | | | | | | | | | | | | | |

Six months after Sir Lancelot had rescued Guinevere, King Arthur received a letter from the pope, in Rome. The pope instructed the king to forgive his queen and take her back, despite her betrayal of him, and to forgive and make his peace with Sir Lancelot.

"You cannot take her back," Sir Gawain told King Arthur. "How can you?"

"I cannot defy the pope," the king replied.

"If you make your peace with Sir Lancelot," Sir Gawain warned him, "you'll be making an enemy of me."

But in the name of his Christian kingdom, and each man and woman and child in Britain, King Arthur knew that he had no choice but to accept the pope's demands.

And when Sir Lancelot and Guinevere were informed of them, they knew they had to accept them too.

"The king is ready to forgive, or at least to set aside, all that has happened," a messenger told them. "Bring the queen to Carlisle in eight days' time and King Arthur will make his peace with you."

"And Sir Gawain?" inquired Sir Lancelot. "Will he also make his peace with me?"

When Sir Lancelot and Queen Guinevere rode into the courtyard of the castle at Carlisle, both of them were wearing white cloth edged with gold. They were accompanied by no fewer than one hundred knights, all of them dressed in green velvet, each carrying an olive branch in his right hand.

As soon as they saw King Arthur, Sir Gawain sitting beside him, they dismounted. Sir Lancelot took the queen's arm and led her forward. Side by side, they knelt before the king.

King Arthur said nothing. Not a word. He sat grave and silent, eyes lowered.

So Sir Lancelot stood up again. "My king," he said, "your queen is as true to you as she has always been. You've been surrounded by filthy liars."

Sir Gawain drew in his breath sharply and glared at Sir Lancelot, but he said nothing.

"If God were not on Queen Guinevere's side," Sir Lancelot continued, "how could I ever have killed twelve armed knights? I've always served you as best I can. And you know, you well know, sire, that I've always been honorable."

"Honorable?" exclaimed Sir Gawain. "False! You're false."

"Where is Sir Mordred?" inquired Sir Lancelot.

"Away!" Sir Gawain snarled. "At Camelot."

"You do surprise me," Sir Lancelot said through clenched teeth. "It's not I——it's Mordred who is false."

Sir Gawain leaped up. "Words words words!" he shouted. "Whatever the king chooses to do, I'll never make my peace with you. You, Lancelot, you've killed my brothers in arms Gareth and Gaheris."

Sir Lancelot bowed his head. "I loved them," he said. "I loved them. I knighted Gareth and I know how he loved me. That smoke . . . That smoke . . . I didn't recognize them. I'll mourn their deaths for as long as I live."

"Fifteen days," Sir Gawain said. "I'll

give you fifteen days, and then I'll follow you. I'll corner you wherever you are and take revenge on you."

"My king . . ." Sir Lancelot protested.

Still King Arthur remained silent.

"If I were you, Lancelot, I'd put as many miles between us as you can," Sir Gawain warned him. "Hundreds of miles. Thousands. Sail to France, and cower there in one of your castles."

Sir Lancelot helped Queen Guinevere to her feet.

"And there wait for me to come and smash the walls down," Sir Gawain threatened him.

Guinevere looked at Lancelot; Lancelot looked at Guinevere. They had eyes only for each other.

Lancelot's words were these: "My lady, the shining fellowship of the Round Table is shattered. I must leave this court and leave my great king. My lady, I must leave you."

He kissed the queen on her right cheek and turned to face the crowd of knights and all the courtiers motionless around them.

"Is there anyone here," Sir Lancelot called out, "is there a single person who dares say that Queen Guinevere has not been true to her husband and our king? If so, let him speak now or forever hold his peace."

No one stepped forward; no one said a word. The only sound in the courtyard was of white doves gulping and cooing.

The stricken king raised his glistening eyes.

Still Sir Lancelot and Queen Guinevere held each other's gaze. Unblinking, they saw straight into each other's heads and hearts. They saw how together they had shared the sixth trial, the trial of love and loyalty, and how in achieving it they had failed it. | | | | | | | | | | | | |

|| THE TRIAL OF THE BLOOD KNOT ||

KING ARTHUR AND MORDRED

King Arthur well knew that the Round Table owed much of its glory to the achievements of Sir Lancelot. He was able to accept, too, the way in which the greatest of his knights loved Guinevere and Guinevere loved him. He had no wish to see Sir Lancelot hounded and banished.

On the other hand, the king certainly didn't want to lose the loyalty of his own nephew Sir Gawain, now the most powerful knight in the kingdom. And he recognized that in order to retain the loyalty of all the knights throughout Britain who were faithful to him, he would have to avenge the deaths of those men slain by Sir Lancelot.

Sir Gawain was able to persuade the reluctant king to raise an army and pursue Sir Lancelot, but because of that, Arthur was obliged by the law of the land to make Sir Mordred, his own treacherous son, regent of the kingdom of Britain while he was away in France.

He knew how jealous Mordred was of him and how he had played his dark part in ambushing Sir Lancelot, while protesting that he was only being loyal to the king. Not only this! For as long as he was abroad, the king was also required to put his wife, Guinevere, in the young regent's care.

Sometimes, thought Arthur, your head and heart point one way but the law points another. I know that's what Merlin would tell me. He would smile that curious, hovering smile of his and say that no one is above the law, least of all the king.

| | | | | | | | | | | | | | | | | | | | | | | | | | | | | | | | | | | | | | |

Sir Blamore . . .

Sir Bleoberis . . .

Sir Galahantine . . .

Sir Villiars . . .

Sir Melias . . .

Sir Palomides . . .

Sir Galahad . . .

To each of those knights to whom he was related by blood, Sir Lancelot gave dukedoms and earldoms and great tracts of land that he owned in France——Armagnac and Foix and Anjou and Provence and Périgord and Pardiac and Normandy.

Then he reinforced the towers and walls of his castle near Benwick, retreated inside them, and refused to come out and attack the armies of the king and Sir Gawain.

"I'll never shed a drop more blood if I can avoid it," he vowed. "I've shed enough already. I'll give as much ground to my king as I can. Peace is far better than battle after battle and war after war."

For six months, King Arthur and Sir Gawain laid siege to Benwick, but they were unable to scale the walls with ladders or break them down with battering rams or undermine them with tunnels, and Sir Lancelot and his army had laid in sufficient provisions and weapons with which to defend themselves.

Every single day, Sir Gawain galloped right up to the walls and challenged Sir Lancelot to joust with him. One morning he shouted, "Where are you, Sir Lancelot? You coward! Trembling in your castle like a rabbit in its hole. You've committed treason. Come out, you coward!"

"I've been hoping that winter would arrive early and cold," Sir Lancelot told his knights, "so cold that Arthur's army would be blowing on their nails and that he'd lift the siege. But I will not be threatened. Not by Sir Gawain. Not by anyone. I'll fight him."

Then the two men exchanged messages. They agreed to fight to the death or until one of them yielded.

Years before, a holy man had endowed Sir Gawain with a magical power. For the three hours before midday, the knight was able to fight with three times his normal strength. When Sir Gawain and Sir Lancelot met, they rained such blows on each other that the legs of their horses gave way beneath them. Then the two knights fought hand to hand. Sir Lancelot was on the very point of having to yield when he noticed that Sir Gawain was no longer as agile as he had been all morning and that his blows were becoming less weighty.

Soon after midday, Sir Lancelot struck Sir Gawain a terrible blow on the side of his helmet. Sir Gawain dropped his sword, dropped his shield, and his legs buckled.

Sir Lancelot stepped back, and Sir Gawain looked up at him. "Why hesitate?" he panted. "Kill me now, Lancelot. Kill me, you traitor!"

"I'm no traitor," Sir Lancelot replied. "No, I will not kill you. I'll never kill a man who is at my mercy and defenseless."

"And I will not submit," Sir Gawain gasped. "If you spare me now, I'll only fight you again."

King Arthur's own doctors laid Sir Gawain on a stretcher and bled him with leeches. They rubbed his wounds with soft ointments, but it was still three weeks before he was well enough to fight again.

As before, Sir Gawain taunted and vexed Sir Lancelot.

"I see now that if ever I lie at your feet, and not you at mine," Sir Lancelot responded, "I must expect no mercy. My days on earth would be at an end."

"Step back now," the king advised his nephew. "You've proven yourself. There's no need for you to fight again."

"Why?" asked Sir Gawain. "Do you think he'll better me?"

King Arthur sighed. "I wish

you both to win and wish neither to lose," he said.

But Sir Gawain wouldn't accept the king's advice, and when he fought for a second time, his strength again waxed for three hours but waned after midday. Then Sir Lancelot felled him with a fearsome swinging blow that reopened his head wound. For a while, Sir Gawain lay unconscious, and when he came around, he waved his sword feebly and told Sir Lancelot to finish him off.

"I won't raise my arm until you can stand on your own feet," Sir Lancelot replied.

"I'll fight you again," Sir Gawain whispered. "Our feud will never end until one of us lies dead."

But just before Sir Lancelot and Sir Gawain were to fight for the third time, a messenger arrived from Britain with horrifying news for them.

"Sir Mordred," the messenger reported, "has told all the great men still left in Britain that you are dead. He's told them that he has received

letters from Sir Gawain and other knights here informing him that you are dead."

King Arthur growled. "Is that so? Dead, am I?"

"Sire, Sir Mordred has announced that Sir Lancelot killed you during this siege. He's obliged many men to name him as their new king, and the archbishop has crowned him at Canterbury. King Mordred!"

"Go on!" said King Arthur in a low, dark voice.

"Your Majesty," continued the messenger, "Sir Mordred rode to Camelot and told your own queen, Guinevere, that he was going to marry her."

King Arthur rounded on the messenger, eyes blazing.

"What?" he shouted.

The messenger shrank but repeated, "Marry her, sire."

"And she agreed?"

"No, sire!"

"Never!" roared the king. "Never!"

"She tricked him, sire. She told

Mordred she needed to go to London to see her dressmakers, and choose accessories for the wedding. But as soon as she got there, she rode straight to the White Tower with many of her courtiers and armed men and walled herself in."

"And then?" barked the king.

"Sir Mordred chased after the queen and besieged her in the tower, but the archbishop rode after Sir Mordred. He accused your son of angering God and bringing shame on the whole order of knighthood. I have his exact words in mind, sire."

The king glared at the messenger.

"The archbishop told Sir Mordred, 'You are King Arthur's son. You can never marry your father's wife, not in this world or the next. If you persist, I will curse you with bell, book, and candle.'

"Then Sir Mordred said to the archbishop, 'You can do what you like. I'm going to marry Guinevere.'"

"Foul!" the king exclaimed. "Filthy!"

The messenger paused. "Then, sire, Sir Mordred grasped his sword and told the archbishop that if he said as much as another word, he'd behead him. I was there myself. I heard him."

King Arthur buried his head in his hands. It's as I feared when I made him my regent, he thought. Worse than I feared. Now Mordred will turn to Morgan for support——she's just as eager to put an end to me as he is. And he'll be telling everyone that my reign has been nothing but one feud after another, betrayal after betrayal, war after war. Many people will listen to him. They'll believe him when he offers them peace. Merlin was right when he warned me that Mordred would one day take vengeance on me because his mother is my own half sister.

King Arthur paced in his tent. I hope with all my head and heart, the king thought, that my own mother, Ygerna, and old Sir Ector and Lady Margery, never hear of all this——this outrage. "Here and now," he declared, "our siege of Benwick is at an end. It is lifted. My army must set off for Britain as soon as it possibly can."

"I believe, sire," the messenger told him, "that Sir Mordred will assemble an army and try to stop you from landing."

"I will stay," Sir Gawain said. "I must finish my fight with Sir Lancelot."

"No," the king replied at once. "Terrible as your feud is, the news from Britain is worse. Far worse. Mordred is a traitor. He's threatening me, threatening my wife, threatening my kingdom. Gawain, I need you to stand beside me."

| | | | | | | | | | | | | | | | | | | | | | | | | | | | | | | | |

Sir Mordred's scouts were keeping watch on the chalk cliffs at Dover, and as soon as they saw King Arthur's huge army crossing the Channel toward them in barges and cobles and fishing smacks, little cockleshells, skiffs, and even rowing boats, they blew conches and trumpets. At once, Sir Mordred's army began to scramble down to the beach, intent on preventing the king from gaining even a foothold in Britain.

So the battle was fought on the shingle, and in and out of the little burbling wavelets, and even on the decks of some of the larger boats.

There was no stopping the king's men. They disembarked and crowded onto the beach, thousands and thousands of them, drumming the pommels of their swords and the butts of their axes against their shields, and before long, Sir Mordred's army was stumbling along the beach, scrambling up the cliffs, wading away through deeper water. Many of them were drowned.

Hundreds of King Arthur's men, too, were killed on the beach at Dover, and the king gave orders that they should be buried under the soft shoulders of the chalk cliffs. After the battle, his boatmen went from craft to craft, lifting dead men out of them, and that's when they found Sir Gawain in a fishing smack. He was still alive, lying on his back, with one leg hooked over a gunwale.

King Arthur took his nephew in his arms. For a long while, he nursed him. The little boat gently rocked, and the small, salty waves washed around them.

"Gawain!" said the king. "Gawain, you're the man I've loved most in this world. And after you, as you must know, I've loved Lancelot. You and Lancelot have given me greater joy than anyone else, and I've always trusted each of you. And now . . . now I've lost you. I've lost you both. Gawain, my Gawain!"

The king's healing words, the clean salty air, the gentle rocking: whatever it was, Sir Gawain revived just a little.

"Uncle," he said, "my head wound, the one Lancelot gave me, has opened again. And this time it will be the death of me." Gawain paused and closed his eyes, and the king thought he was gone forever. But then he opened his eyes again. "I know it is I who caused this conflict, this terrible feud. For as long as Sir Lancelot was standing beside you, no one whatsoever dared to oppose you."

Again Sir Gawain closed his eyes, and then he murmured, "Uncle, have one of your scribes bring me pen and ink and parchment."

I, Sir Gawain, greet you, Sir Lancelot. I have come to my death day because of my head wound. Before I die, I want it known that it was I who would not make peace with you. You would have willingly made peace with me.

Sir Lancelot, remember how close we were once, you and I, how much we cared for each other. I beg you, come and save our king. His foul son, Sir Mordred, has had himself crowned and tried to force himself on Queen Guinevere. We have landed at Dover, fought hundreds of his men, and sent them scurrying away like rats, but Sir Mordred still has the country in his grip.

I've counseled the king to offer Mordred land and rewards and a treaty for a month, and on no account to engage with him again, but to wait, Sir Lancelot, until you come and fight beside him. When I have died, I will visit the king in his dreams and again warn him to wait. To wait for you.

Sir Gawain sighed and took a deep, deep breath——as deep as life itself. Then he closed his eyes again, and this time, he did not open them again.

|||||||||||||||||||||||||||||||||||

Two weeks passed while King Arthur and Sir Mordred exchanged angry messages. And then, somewhere southwest of the holy city of Salisbury, high on the sweeping downs patrolled by armies of scudding clouds, King Arthur negotiated with his loathsome son.

He appointed Sir Lucan and Sir Bedivere and two bishops to speak on his behalf, and for three days, they and Sir Mordred's representatives talked and argued. The outcome was that the king's son would take immediate control of Kent and Cornwall and that, after King Arthur's death, he would be crowned king of the whole of England.

"I'm not at all satisfied with this arrangement," King Arthur told his knights. "How could I possibly be? But at least all this back-and-forth and arguing is done with."

King Arthur consented to meet Sir Mordred face to face on neutral green ground between the pounding armies. Each was accompanied by just fourteen men, so that they could sign and witness the agreement and drink a beaker of wine together as a sign of their good faith.

"Keep watch," the king told his leaders. "Don't take your eyes off us for a moment. Mordred's as slippery as a snake. If you see any of his men draw a sword, gallop over to us full tilt and kill Mordred. He's a traitor."

Likewise, Sir Mordred warned his men. "Keep watch. I know my father hates me, and the terms of our treaty aren't worth the parchment they're written on. He'll try to take revenge on me. If you see anyone with him draw a his sword, gallop straight over and kill King Arthur and everyone with him."

Then the two groups of men began to walk slowly across the springy turf toward each other.

Scattered across the downs were little prickly gorse bushes, their flowers almost as bright-eyed as the night

stars. Out of one bush oozed an adder, unseen by anyone. It sidled across the cropped grass and bit one of Sir Mordred's followers on his right foot.

The knight yelled and drew his sword, meaning to cut the snake in half. At once, the leaders of both armies saw the shining blade and gave the signal to their men. Trumpets blared and drums banged and horns blew. Then the two armies engaged, with King Arthur and Sir Mordred right in the thick of them.

Of all the battles that have ever reddened and rusted British earth, this was the most cruel. It was the trial of the blood knot, and set father against son and son against father, brother against brother, Englishman against Englishman. From mid-morning until early evening, that hour when the sun begins to set and the moon is already riding high: eight hours of spear thrust, sword swing, shield song, ax hack, staff jab, and knife cut; eight hours of boasts and insults and shouts and screams and groans; suffocating

sweat and bleeding bodies; bloated flies, croaking ravens.

The battlefield grew dim and quiet. On that single day, one hundred thousand men lost their lives.

When King Arthur no longer had to fend off one attacker after another, he stared at the darkening sky, then stared around him, and realized that only two, only two of his great host of knights were left standing. His butler, Sir Lucan, and one-armed Sir Bedivere. Both men were badly wounded.

"Where are you all?" the king called out. "My brave friends, my good friends. Where?" The king paused. "It's over. Almost over . . . but how I wish I knew where Sir Mordred was. My own son. He's the root of all this ghastly slaughter, all this evil."

Then King Arthur saw his son. He was leaning heavily on his sword as if it were a staff, surrounded by a gruesome heap of dead men.

"Give me my spear," Arthur told Sir Lucan.

"No, sire," said his butler. "Let Sir

Mordred be. Every single one of his men lies dead. He can never threaten you or your kingdom again."

"My spear," the king insisted.

"Remember Sir Gawain's warning, sire. Wait until Sir Lancelot comes and fights beside you."

"I won't let him escape," King Arthur growled. "Whether I live or die, I won't."

Then the king leveled his spear and ran straight at his son, shouting, "You traitor! Traitor! Are you ready to die?"

King Arthur drove the wicked point deep into his son's body just above his black shield, and Sir Mordred knew at once that his wound was fatal. He thrust his body forward, until the spear was sticking right out of his back, so as to be able to reach his father. He whirled his sword and struck King Arthur on the side of the head and pierced his father's brainpan.

Sir Mordred gave an almighty howl of defiance and defeat, and fell over sideways, stone dead.

|||||||||||||||||||||||||||||||||||||

Dazed but not unconscious, less awake than drifting, the king swam between worlds.

Between them, Sir Lucan and Sir Bedivere managed to half walk, half drag him a little way from the battlefield, as far as a peaceful chapel. It stood high on the downs, above the lake where the king had first won Excalibur.

There the three men rested until they were disturbed by yells and cries from the battlefield.

"No!" the king moaned, and he tried to raise his hands so as to cover his ears. "No, not again."

"No, sire," Sir Lucan reassured him. "All your enemies are dead."

"Their spirits, then?" King Arthur inquired. "Their ghosts are ready to lead me to my grave."

"No, sire," said Sir Bedivere.

Sir Lucan walked back up to the battlefield to discover the reason for the noise, and in the moonlight, the knight saw that corpse robbers were doing their grisly work, ripping armor and brooches and rings from dead

men, while ravens croaked and pecked at them. Worse, whenever they found any luckless knight badly wounded but still alive, they swore and cut his throat, and then stole anything worthwhile from him.

"You're not safe here," Sir Lucan told the king when he returned. "We must try to get you away."

"I can't even stand," King Arthur said, and he took a deep breath. "I'm so lightheaded. Ah! If only . . ."

"Sire?"

"Sir Lancelot! Why did I ever agree to pursue you to France? Lancelot, with you beside me, I know I would have lived; without you, I must die."

"Sire," said Sir Bedivere, "do not doubt that as soon as he received Sir Gawain's message, Sir Lancelot set off for Britain to fight beside you."

"Too late!" murmured the king. "I should have waited until he came, as Sir Gawain counseled me."

Then Sir Lucan raised the king's head and shoulders, and Sir Bedivere wrapped his one arm around the king's legs, and they lifted him. But almost at once, Sir Lucan moaned and collapsed. Foaming at the mouth, he died beside his king.

King Arthur mourned his loyal butler. "He needed more help than I," he groaned, "yet he was still ready to help me."

Sir Bedivere sat with the king on the sweet grass, already damp with dew. His head was bowed and his arm was wrapped around his knees. From time to time, he shook but said nothing.

"I believe . . ." began the king.

"Sire?"

"Bedivere, I believe I've little time left."

Sir Bedivere could hear how heavily the king was breathing.

"Excalibur," he murmured. "Excalibur . . . Morgan never gave me back your scabbard as she said she would." The king paused. To Bedivere, he said, "Take my sword down to the lake and throw it in. Then come straight back to me and tell me what you saw."

Sir Bedivere got to his feet. "I will do as you ask," he said.

On his way down, Sir Bedivere saw for the first time how Excalibur's pommel and haft were exquisitely inlaid with rubies and emeralds and sapphires and diamonds.

"What good can come of throwing this sword away?" he asked himself. "None. None at all," he answered.

So he hid Excalibur beside the trunk of an old oak tree.

"What did you see?" King Arthur asked Bedivere when he returned.

"Nothing but wind ripples and little waves, sire."

The king shook his head and sighed. "I do not believe you," he said. "Go straight back and do as I've asked you. Bedivere, I've always trusted you."

Sir Bedivere walked back down to the oak tree and picked up Excalibur.

It would be quite wrong, he thought again, wrong and even sinful to throw away this precious sword. So he hid it for a second time.

"What did you see?" King Arthur asked him when he once again returned.

"Sire, nothing but the waters wap and the waves wan."

"Ah, Bedivere! Who in this world would ever believe that you'd disobey and betray me, all for a few jewels on the pommel of my sword?" The king was panting. "Hurry, now! Hurry! My arms, my feet, my legs, they're growing cold. If you betray me for a third time, and I'm still alive when you come back, I'll . . . I'll stand up and wring your neck."

Sir Bedivere hurried down to the oak tree for the third and final time. He

picked up the sword, strode to the water's edge, and hurled it out as far as he could.

And by the light of the forgiving moon, the knight saw a white hand and arm rising out of the lake——rising and catching the sword by its pommel, three times shaking it and holding it up to high heaven, and then sinking, vanishing into the night water.

Sir Bedivere hurried back to his king and told him what he had seen.

"Now," whispered the king, "carry me down to the water."

The knight hoisted King Arthur onto his broad back, and when they reached the bank of the lake, a little barge loomed out of the darkness, rowed by eight oarsmen.

Six ladies, all wearing black hooded cloaks, were sitting in it. Upon seeing Sir Bedivere carrying the king, they began to weep.

"Put me in the barge," the king told Sir Bedivere.

The knight gently laid him out along a thwart with his head in the lap of one of the ladies, then stepped back to shore.

The oarsmen were ready, and Sir Bedivere called out, "My king! My lord! What will become of me?"

But King Arthur did not answer him.

"My king!" Sir Bedivere cried out again. "What will become of me now that you're leaving me? Now that I'm alone and still with so many enemies?"

"Be calm," the king counseled him. "Find what strength you can in your own head and your own heart. I can help you no longer."

The oarsmen leaned forward and braced their backs.

"I will cross to Avalon," King Arthur told Sir Bedivere, "and there my earthly wounds will heal. Pray for me. And if you hear no more of me, pray for my soul."

"Arthur!" called Sir Bedivere. "You cannot die. You cannot."

In the barge, all the ladies were sobbing.

"Arthur!" the knight called across the dark and shining water. "You will live forever, our always king!"

|||||||||||||||||||||||||||||||||||||

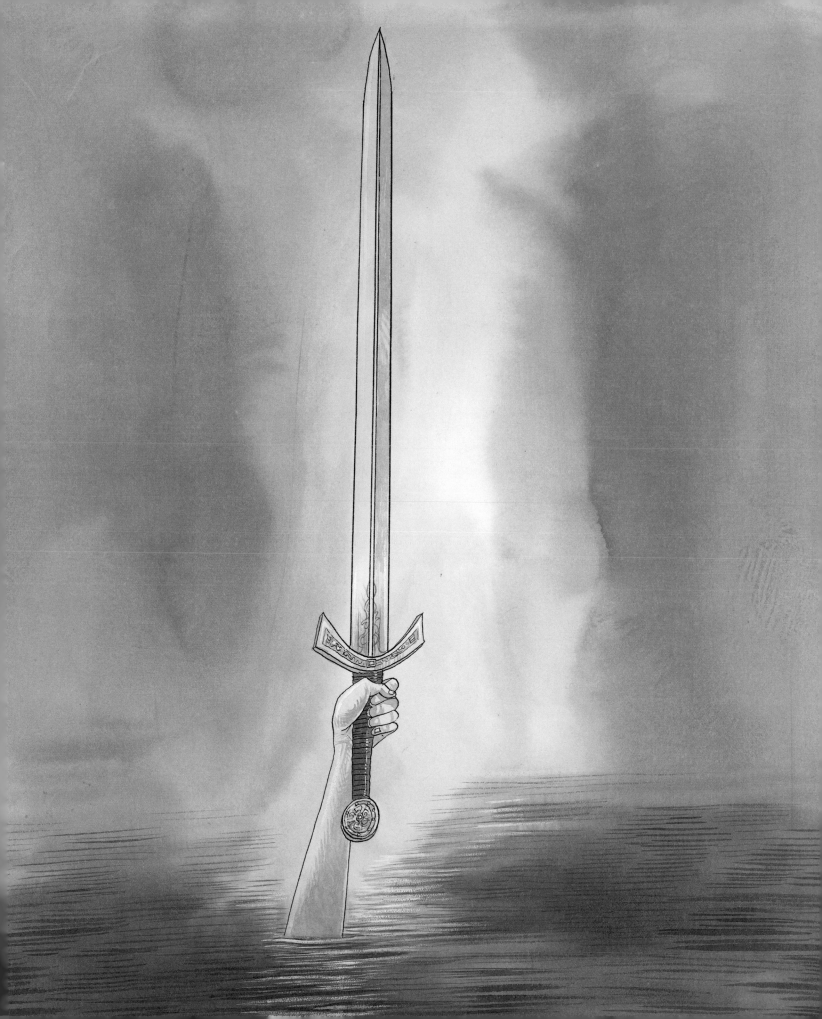

XI

‖ MERLIN IN HIS HOUSE OF GLASS ‖

Merlin saw all this.

He saw the appalling battle between King Arthur and his own son. He saw Sir Bedivere hurl Excalibur into the lake, where a white hand caught and brandished it. He saw the knight carry the king down to the barge and heard their last words to each other.

Wheresoever he was, Merlin could see and hear everything.

His apprentice, Nimue, had no wish ever to see the old enchanter again, and so she had abandoned him in the dripping cave draped with spiderwebs, where she had imprisoned him.

Then, after seven years, she spirited him to a house of glass, out at sea or beyond the sea. From there the magi-cian was able to watch and listen, and from there he listens and watches still.

In his house of glass, Merlin is guarding thirteen treasures:

A cloak of invisibility.

A sword that bursts into flame if one tries to draw it from its scabbard.

A drinking horn always full to the brim, no matter how much one drinks from it.

A chariot.

A whetstone.

A platter always charged with what-ever one wishes to eat.

A red gown.

A hamper.

A knife with which to make living sacrifices.

A cauldron.

A golden chessboard with silver pieces that play themselves.

A mantle that always warms its wearer even in the most freezing weather.

A ring to wear when one wants to see without being seen.

These are the thirteen treasures of the island of Britain that Merlin guards.

Days and months pass. Seasons pass; years pass.

Merlin narrows his eyes. He looks through space. He looks backward and forward through time.

He sees the Jewish trader, Joseph of Arimathea, sailing from the Holy Land, bringing with him the Holy Grail, the chalice used by Jesus and His disciples at the Last Supper.

Merlin blinks.

He sees a man called Arthur fighting alongside four Cornish kings and driving out a party of Vikings who overstayed their welcome——not that they were in the least welcome to begin with! They've fathered red-haired babies with Cornish girls, and choughs and kittiwakes have nested in the rigging of their ships.

He can see a Welsh leader called Arthur who, like Merlin himself, is able to cross between worlds. Members of his war band have supernatural powers. One man is able to walk along the tips of grass blades, and another can drop his lower lip down to his navel and toss his upper lip over his head like a helmet.

Again Merlin blinks.

He sees himself carrying a baby boy, only two or three days old, away from the clifftop castle at Tintagel. And he sees Arthur and Kay as they grow up, and sees Arthur, aged fifteen, walking into Saint Paul's churchyard and pulling the sword from the stone.

He sees the stricken king lying in a barge with his head in a lady's lap, crossing to Avalon.

Merlin blinks.

He sees monks at Glastonbury Abbey laughing and digging a fake grave, lowering into it the bones of an enormous man, a giant almost, with a fractured skull, and the bones of a woman with a wave of red-gold hair. He sees the monks laying a lead cross over them inscribed HIC IACET SEPULTUS (here lies buried) INCLITUS REX ARTURIUS (the renowned King Arthur) IN INSULA AVALONIA (in the island of Avalon).

Merlin sees the monks wiping their brows and gaily chattering about how they'll pretend to discover the fake grave they've just dug, and soon attract thousands of pilgrims to the abbey and get rich.

The magician purses his old mouth and blinks.

Merlin watches the Bishop of Winchester go hunting in the forest nearby, the one that stretches over Sleepers Hill. He watches as the bishop is separated from his companions and comes to a palace he has never seen before. The king who lives there invites him to dinner, and the bishop asks him his name.

"Arthur," says the king. "King Arthur."

"King Arthur!" exclaims the bishop. "The king who long ago ruled all of Britain?"

"The same," says the king.

"But who will believe me?" the bishop asks him. "Who will ever believe I've seen and spoken to King Arthur?"

"Close your right hand," the king tells him.

The bishop closes his right hand.

"Now open it," says the king.

And out flutters a butterfly! Out and up and away!

"For as long as you live," says the king, "you'll be able to do this. If anyone doubts that you met me, just close and then open your right hand. You can tell them that it was my gift to you."

The old magician smiles. And he blinks again.

Merlin watches two children, sister and brother, exploring near the Rock of the Fortress in the mountains north of Swansea.

He watches them discover a cave, and disappear into it, and walk along a gloomy tunnel, and duck their heads under a bell-shaped rock, and reach a rough stony platform overlooking a great chamber——a hall decorated with stalagmites and stalactites.

The children gaze down, and in the chamber they see hundreds of knights, sleeping——and King Arthur himself, still young, King Arthur sleeping in the middle of them.

One knight is snoring, one turns from side to side, one is babbling in his sleep. They do not wake. Very deep is their slumber around their Sleeping Lord.

For a long while, the children stare, but at last they quietly turn away.

Neither of them sees the bell-shaped rock, not until the boy bumps his forehead right into it. The sound of the collision rings in the children's ears, and it rings through the rock chamber, and it rings around the world.

At once, there's a clamor. Several of the knights wake and jump up and chase after the two children, shouting, "Is it the day? Is it the day?"

Out again beneath the white sky, and only just in time, the girl and boy are scared, dazed, thrilled . . .

Merlin nods to himself, and he blinks again.

"In my glass house," he vows. "I will guard the thirteen treasures. I will guard them until the day that is the day: the day King Arthur wakes again and reclaims the island of Britain.

"This story," murmurs the magician, "and all the stories within it, is a kind of unending dream, an imagining.

"Is it a way with words?

"A way of understanding? A way of life?" ||||||||||||||||||||||||||||

ACKNOWLEDGMENTS

My service at Camelot has been a long one, and while I was writing my Arthur trilogy, many people helped me to interpret the legends, notably Judith Elliott and distinguished medievalists and Arthurian scholars Richard Barber and Nigel Bryant. I have also been supported by a wonderful team at Walker Books, spearheaded by my éditrice sans pareille, Denise Johnstone-Burt, and Ben Norland, finest of art directors, as well as by Alice Primmer, Louisa Dinwiddie, Meera Santiapillai, and Ellen Abernethy. Thanks too to Mary Lee Donovan and Juan Botero for their careful suggestions adapting the text for an American reader. I must also thank my excellent agent, Hilary Delamere; Karen Clarke for so patiently preparing numerous versions of these tales; and my eagle-eyed and discerning wife, Linda, for her editorial suggestions. To work in tandem with Chris Riddell has been a very great privilege and pleasure.

||||||||||||||||||||||||||||||||||||||||||||||||||||||||

Text copyright © 2021 by Kevin Crossley-Holland • Illustrations copyright © 2021 by Chris Riddell • All rights reserved. No part of this book may be reproduced, transmitted, or stored in an information retrieval system in any form or by any means, graphic, electronic, or mechanical, including photocopying, taping, and recording, without prior written permission from the publisher. • First US edition 2023 • Library of Congress Catalog Card Number 2021953316 • ISBN 978-1-5362-1265-5 • This book was typeset in Fell Type Historical. The illustrations were done in ink, pastel pencil, and watercolor. Candlewick Studio, an imprint of Candlewick Press, 99 Dover Street, Somerville, Massachusetts 02144 • www.candlewickstudio.com

Printed in Shenzhen, Guangdong, China 23 24 25 26 27 28 CCP 10 9 8 7 6 5 4 3 2 1